RULE #7 YOU CAN'T FAKE DATE YOUR BROTHER'S BEST FRIEND

THE RULES OF LOVE BOOK 7

ANNE-MARIE MEYER

Copyright © 2019 by Anne-Marie Meyer

All rights reserved.

No part of this book may be reproduced in any form or by any electronic or mechanical means, including information storage and retrieval systems, without written permission from the author, except for the use of brief quotations in a book review.

For my Family

"My grandfather taught me to hold doors and pay for women's food." He paused before meeting my gaze. "And I'm more terrified of him haunting me from the grave than you and your adorable little scowl."

BLAKE

1

SUSIE

My room smelled like sage.

Well், burning sage would be the accurate term.

The smell and the sound of Mom's feet shuffling around on the plush new carpet of our new ranch in Montana told me one thing: she was cleansing my room.

"Ma," I mumbled as I flipped to my stomach and buried my face into my pillow. "Did you have to do this at the crack of dawn?" I tipped my head slightly to the side so I could yawn without suffocating myself and then buried my nose deep into the fluff in the hope of muting out the smell.

"We can't live here with bad spirits," Mom sang out. Her voice shifted around me.

I groaned and pushed myself up. So much for sleeping. "You're crazy, you know that?"

Mom was standing near the window, making circles with the smoke that was billowing from the sage bundle she was clutching. She had a multicolored scarf wrapped around her head and a pinkish hue to her cheeks. A sight that I had missed ever since she started chemotherapy four months ago.

It made me wonder if today was going to be a good day.

She seemed to be oblivious to my stares. Instead, she chuckled as she moved to stand next to the bed and then leaned over to bop me on the nose. "If it keeps my family safe, I'll be as crazy as I need to be."

I playfully glared at her, but that only lasted for a moment before my frown morphed into a soft smile. I knew that Mom hated it when we looked at her with sorrow, but it was hard not to. Stage four cancer wasn't something most women came back from. The more time marched on, the less time I feared I had with her.

Not wanting my worry to get the best of me, I sighed and brought my knees up to my chest to hug them. Moving to Glories Bluff, Montana hadn't been on my bucket list, but when Dad got the job as the town's veterinarian and Mom found the house on forty acres with a huge willow tree that hung over the pond, I knew I couldn't fight my parents. They were just too darn happy to make the move. And happiness was in short supply in our family.

They'd always wanted to move out of New York, and

time to make it happen was quickly coming to an end. We were determined to live our lives to the fullest with whatever we had left with Mom. Even if that meant pulling Paul and me out of our junior and senior year of high school to achieve that happiness.

I, however, was indifferent. Besides desperately wanting to see a smile on Mom's face every morning, it sucked to leave my friends and life that I had behind me when we moved. Sure, I wasn't your typical high school popular girl, but that didn't mean I didn't have friends.

All three of said friends were crushed when I told them my family was moving, but they knew why we were making the change. Alison, Cameron, and Paisley promised to keep in touch—which I wasn't holding my breath about. Long distance relationships never seemed to work out.

Besides, Mom was happy, and for the first time in a month, she looked happy. I would trade all of my friends for this opportunity to sit on my mattress and watch Mom dance happily around me.

I never wanted this to change.

Mom stopped circling around me, dragging the burning sage in front of her so that the smoke drifted across the room and faced me. "I think I'm done here." She smiled. "I'm going to go cleanse Paul's room and then get started on breakfast."

I wanted to fight her about doing too much. Tell her that she really should lay down and rest after she cleansed

Paul's room, but I didn't want to see the downturned look that was sure to follow my words. Mom so badly wanted to take care of us that I couldn't burst her bubble like this. So, I yawned and stretched. "Sounds good."

"Bacon and eggs?"

My mouth watered at the words. "You know it." I'd just make sure to hurry getting ready, so I could come down and help her.

Mom was almost out the door before she stopped. "How does your room feel?" she asked. I could hear her excitement in her voice.

Not wanting to disappoint her, I nodded. "Completely different."

"Har har."

I winked. "I mean it."

She playfully glowered before her eyebrows raised. "Before I forget, Blake's coming over this morning, so..." She waggled her finger in my direction. "Make sure you are dressed and have a bra on."

My arms wrapped protectively around my chest. "Ma," I said, my cheeks heating.

"I know, he's your brother's best friend since they were in diapers, but he's a man now. And you are—"

"I get it. I get it." There was no way I was going to sit here and suffer through another sex-ed conversation with Mom that involved a plug and outlet. That was horrifying and scarring when I was eight, and I had a sinking suspicion that it wouldn't be any better at sixteen. "I'll get dressed," I said.

Mom nodded and after a moment, slipped out into the hallway, shutting my door behind her. I sighed as I stretched out my legs. Butterflies floated around in my stomach as I thought back on her words.

Blake and my brother Paul had been friends forever. Both my family and the Marshalls lived in the same apartment building in Brooklyn before Brett Marshall inherited his grandfather's ranch here in Montana and the family picked up and moved.

While it had been a few years since I last saw the Marshalls, Paul and Blake worked at the dude ranch just outside of Glories Bluff every summer for the last three years. So when Dad floated the idea of leaving New York to move here for Paul's senior year, my brother had no objection.

We were packed up and heading across the country in a matter of months.

Even though I hadn't seen Blake face to face, I saw pictures of him at the ranch standing alongside Paul. He'd gotten taller and was definitely filled out. And from what I could tell by all the girls that were hanging on his arm—he knew it.

Which just made everything much worse. The kid I remembered who made me mud pies and spun me on the trap of death on the playground until I almost puked was

Blake. A very grown up and handsome Blake. Pictures did not do him justice.

Crap.

He smiled at me, but there was a sheepish hint to his expression. He shrugged as he held up the knife. "You looked like you were struggling."

I wanted to crawl into a hole and die. Here I was, standing in the middle of the living room, wrapped in a blanket and dripping water everywhere. I knew enough about myself to know that I looked more like a drowned rat than a lifeguard on any Hollywood movie.

This was not how I wanted my first meeting with Blake to go.

"Thanks," was all I could muster as I watched Blake focus his attention on cutting the tape.

He pulled open the flaps and glanced inside. "I'm guessing this was what you were looking for," he said as he pulled out a white towel and handed it to me.

"Yeah, thanks," I repeated as I grabbed the towel and hugged it to my chest. Before he or I could say anything more, I kept my head down and hurried to the stairs.

Once I was inside my room, I shut my door and then flopped onto my mattress. I covered my eyes with my arm as the memory of staring into Blake's eyes flashed through my mind.

That was a fail.

It took a minute before I felt brave enough to peel myself off my unmade bed and face my reflection in the mirror. I dried off and slipped into a pair of jean shorts and a plain yellow t-shirt. After towel drying and then brushing my hair, I braided it back and then applied some lip gloss and mascara.

My cheeks were still pink from our encounter, but I just hoped it made me look like I'd applied blush instead of experiencing a completely embarrassing moment just minutes ago.

I could hear voices downstairs when I pulled open my door. I contemplated running back into my room and never coming out, but I knew that there was a high likelihood that Mom would send Blake up here to get me, and I wanted to avoid that catastrophe. I just shut my door quietly behind me and headed back down the hall.

I was going to hope that Mom would be so wrapped up in talking to Blake that she wouldn't notice me and therefore wouldn't draw any attention my direction.

Even though I knew that was a slim possibility, I was still going to hope.

"Oh good, you're dressed and here," Mom said the moment I stepped into the kitchen.

I just nodded and moved to sit down at the far end of the table.

"Susanne Jordan, don't be rude."

I paused before I glanced up. Mom was standing next to the stove with a spatula in hand. Blake was leaning against the counter with his gaze trained on me while he munched on a piece of bacon.

"I'm sorry, Mom," I whispered, not really sure how I was being rude and not really wanting to continue this conversation.

"You didn't greet our guest," Mom said as she waved her spatula in Blake's direction.

Out of instinct, my gaze drifted over to him. "Hello," I said and then cringed at how formal I sounded.

Blake's eyebrows went up. "Hello."

There was a silence that fell around us. I glanced from Blake to Mom, hoping that someone would save me from this awkward experience.

Thankfully, it didn't take Mom too long to sputter and then turn to flip her eggs. "That was the driest reunion I've ever seen," she said as she plated the eggs.

"We talked earlier," Blake said.

My gaze whipped over to him. What was he doing? Where was he going with this?

"Oh really?" Mom asked as she handed over the plate with eggs to Blake.

He nodded. "I helped her get out a towel."

"Blake," I hissed. I wasn't sure how Mom was going to take that, but there was one thing Cheryl Jordan had along with her daughter, and that was an overactive imagination. In a matter of seconds, Mom was going to see romance, wedding bells, and grandkids.

And those were the kinds of things that she should say to me, and me only.

"Towel?" Mom asked with a frown.

He nodded as he shoveled some eggs into his mouth, blatantly ignoring the death stares I was sending his direction. "She needed me to open a box."

Mom paused but then nodded. "Well, that's sweet of you to help our little Susie. I'm sure she's grateful."

Despite the fact that my mother called me little Susie, I felt grateful. Blake made no mention of my attire or just showered look. To mom, he'd just helped me. We were going to keep it at that.

I wanted to get up and help Mom finish breakfast, but I was cemented to my seat. The last thing I needed was to remind Mom that I was there, thus spurring further intrusive comments.

Plus, Mom looked perfectly content flipping the popping bacon, and I would be a liar if I said I wasn't enjoying just watching her be her for once. I already had images of Mom losing her hair and throwing up over the toilet. I needed to replace them with something positive.

Blake seemed happy to chat with Mom. It was as if our families had never been apart. He ate, and she asked questions. They definitely got along well.

"Are you dating anyone?"

Mom's question came so fast that I hadn't prepared myself for it. I inhaled as the last words hit my ears, which sent me into a coughing fit. Blake and Mom turned their attention to me, and I held up my hand as I reached for my water. My eyes were watering, but I would survive this.

The last thing I needed was for them to come to my rescue.

Blake drew his attention back to Mom as I guzzled my water. "I did. Her name's Hannah. But we broke up a week ago." His shoulders sagged.

Rage rose up inside of me. Who was this Hannah, and why did she break Blake's heart? I had half a mind to demand to know who she was so I could give her a piece of my mind. I was fiercely protective over my family. An outgrowth of watching a family member struggle.

"She sounds like a loser," Mom said, the same rage I felt inside shining across her countenance.

Blake chuckled. "Yeah. But I miss her."

Mom shook her head. "You're better without her."

I nodded as I slipped a forkful of eggs into my mouth. Go, Mom.

"I don't know." Blake looked forlorn. "She was pretty perfect for me."

I scoffed which drew Blake's attention over, so I masked my reaction with a cough as if I were still struggling. His gaze rested on me for a moment before he turned back to Mom.

"Well, if she doesn't know your worth, then she's not worth your time." Mom reached over and patted Blake's shoulder.

He nodded and smiled. "Thanks."

Right then, Paul walked into the room. His eyes were bloodshot, and his hair stuck up on one side of his head.

He squinted as he glanced around. "Were you in my room, Ma?" he asked as he pushed his hand through his hair. "It smells weird."

"That's sage, and yes, I was in there." She lifted her spatula up to wiggle it in Paul's direction. "You should thank me. There were some weird spirits in there."

Paul stared at Mom for a moment before he leaned forward and kissed her on the cheek. The rest of the family didn't believe in this mumbo jumbo that Mom always talked about, but we loved her anyway.

"Thanks," he said as she handed him a plate.

"Of course. Anything for my babies."

Paul nodded toward the hallway, and Blake pushed off the counter. Just before he disappeared through the doorway after Paul, he paused. "Thanks, Mrs. Jordan, for the food." Then his gaze drifted over to me, and he smiled. "It was good to see you, Susie."

I smiled and nodded, hating the fact that I blushed from his smile.

What was wrong with me?

"Anytime." Mom's smile faded, and a rock settled in my gut. It was the same thing that happened every time we thought about the future.

Was it there? How much of it did we have left?

Blake just winked at Mom and disappeared, leaving the two of us alone. Mom busied herself around the kitchen, cleaning up. She looked tired, so I stood and took the plate that she was bringing to the sink and set it inside.

"Go lay down. I'll finish cleaning up."

Mom hesitated, and I prepared myself for a fight, but then she stopped and nodded. "That's probably a good idea." I watched her walk from the kitchen over to the living room where she grabbed a throw blanket and pillow and laid down.

My heart ached at the sight in front of me. I hated seeing her like this. If I could, I would take her pain away.

But I was only human. It was a frustrating place to be.

All I knew was I would do anything to make Mom happy.

Anything.

2

SUSIE

Mom slept the rest of the afternoon. I checked on her occasionally, and she was sound asleep, cuddled up on her bed. By the time three o'clock rolled around, I headed into the kitchen. Dad texted that he was picking up a pizza and asked if I could start the oven.

I stared forlornly at the inside of the fridge. I wished we had something to go along with the pizza. Moving across the country caused us to eat out often, and I was ready to eat something colored, anything but tan.

A salad would be nice. Or some carrots.

"Did you lose something in there?"

I yelped and turned to see Blake walk into the kitchen. He had his hands shoved deep into his pockets and a half smile playing on his lips. His hair was tousled which was only amplified when he pulled his hand out of his pocket and pushed his fingers through it once more. As if he knew it was unkempt.

"I'm just wishing I were magical and could make some salad appear." I opened the fridge door further so he could see inside. "We haven't gone grocery shopping."

Blake glanced past me to the fridge and then back over to meet my gaze. He pulled some keys out of his front pocket. "I could take you to Harts."

"Harts?"

"It's the local grocery store around here."

I glanced back in the fridge and then sighed, shutting the doors and turning. "If it's my only option," I said softly as I grabbed my purse from the counter.

He chuckled. "Well, I'm willing to stand there and wait with you to conjure up something" —he leaned closer to me just as I passed by him— "but I have a feeling it's going to take a while."

I paused, the warmth of his breath and the softness of his voice caused me to freeze. A shiver rushed down my back, and I turned to face him. He was smiling like he'd just told the funniest joke. My gaze met his, and butterflies zoomed through my stomach.

Did he feel it too? This…connection between us?

I shook my head. What was I going on about? I'd officially gone crazy.

"You don't want to go?" His expression dropped.

I furrowed my brow. "What?" And then I realized what he thought my head shake meant. I waved my hand in his direction as if I were trying to erase what I'd done. "Oh, no. Not that."

He looked even more confused at my attempt to explain.

"I just had a stupid thought that I was trying to shake loose." I took a step back, putting distance between us so my head could clear. "I definitely need to go to the store." I held up my purse.

Blake studied me as if he didn't believe me but then nodded. "Okay." He pointed toward the hallway. "I'm going to let Paul know we're heading out."

I stayed rooted in my spot and pinched my lips. I gave him a slight nod, and he walked past me.

Once he was out of the kitchen, I sighed and let my body slump against the counter. What was wrong with me? I must be having a brain aneurysm or something. I was officially going crazy.

I needed to keep my thoughts about Blake quiet. He was my brother's friend and that was it. Plus, I was fairly certain that once I saw the other guys at Glories Bluff High, I was going to forget all about Blake.

He was my only option right now. No wonder my mind was running in circles.

When Blake got back, he motioned toward the front door, and I followed. Once outside, I walked over to his blue Honda, and he pulled open the passenger door before I could reach for the handle. I paused, not used to this treatment at all.

I sucked in my breath. "He can definitely hyper focus."

"Yeah. I'm discovering that."

I glanced over at him. "Do you play?"

"Video games?"

I nodded.

He shook his head. "A little. I get bored easily."

"Me, too."

Silence fell between us. I peeked over at him to see that he was resting his wrist on the wheel while leaning his elbow on the console between us. This movement brought him closer to me. That realization sent goosebumps down my arm.

"So, what do you do—"

"What do you do—"

We both stopped talking, pinching our lips together.

"You go first."

"You go first."

This conversation was going nowhere.

I extended out my flat hand in hopes that he would see that as an invitation for him to speak first. He glanced over at me and then nodded.

"I don't know. Sports. Hanging out with friends. Stuff like that."

I wondered if he would have added, hanging with Hannah, to that list if they hadn't just broken up. "That's it?"

He shrugged. "A few other things here and there, but that's the bulk of it."

A few things here and there? That comment flip-flopped in my mind. I wanted to press him for more but decided against it. If he was being purposely vague, I wasn't going to push him.

Silence filled the car once more. Until I saw him glance over at me one too many times. I turned to meet his gaze only to find him looking expectantly at me.

"What?"

He raised his eyebrows. "You heard my life story, now it's your turn."

I narrowed my eyes. "Except you gave me all the boring answers you give during every *get to know you* game."

He dropped his jaw. "I did not." He moved his hand to his chest and clutched it there. "I gave you heartfelt answers."

I snorted. "Did not."

He paused. "What do you want to know?" His voice had deepened.

He had secrets; I could tell from his reaction. I wondered for a brief moment if he would tell them to me... but then I brushed that off.

I was an idiot to entertain those thoughts.

"Something you wouldn't tell anyone." Not wanting this to go too deep, I replied in a playful way.

"If I share, you'll share?"

I glanced over at him. He'd pulled into the parking lot of Harts by now and was idling the engine. He'd turned to face me head on. His gaze startled me.

I swallowed. "What do you want to know?" How had our conversation turned this deep? Sure, I grew up with the kid, but that had been a few years ago. He was foreign to me. There was no way I was going to tell him my deepest darkest secrets. And I doubted he'd tell me his.

We sat in silence for a few moments more before he chuckled and shook his head. "Don't look so serious, little Susie." And those words morphed into The Everly Brother's lyrics, Wake up Little Susie. A song that always accompanies my name.

I sighed as I followed him out of the car. Why I ever thought he wanted to get to know me on a deeper level was beyond me. I was officially crazy to think I could have anything but a kid sister relationship with Blake.

It was my mistake to even think it.

Just as we headed to the entrance, a group of kids who looked as if they were our age rounded the corner. They all greeted Blake who replied back, but he seemed distracted. He was staring at the corner of the store like it owed him money.

Not wanting him to feel obligated to come into the store with me, I said, "I'll meet you out here when I'm done?"

He nodded. "Sounds good."

I walked through the sliding doors and into the ice-cold air conditioning without looking back. Blake's body language made it pretty clear that he didn't want to be seen with me. Which was okay. After all, I was the nerdy new girl.

I was used to guys running the other way when I came around.

I pushed the cart around the store, picking up essentials. Salad, veggies, fruit. Thirty minutes later, the groceries were packed in white plastic bags, and the wheels of the shopping cart made a clanging sound as I rolled over the rails of the sliding glass door.

I squinted against the bright sun as I glanced around for Blake. He was leaning against his car with his head down. He was staring at his hands and occasionally dusting them off before inspecting them again.

I sighed as I started pushing the groceries toward him. How was it that one simple act made him look so...handsome? Was this what I was destined to feel for the next year? Was I attracted to Blake?

I shook my head, dropping my gaze to the ground and cursing myself for even thinking those words. Once they were in my mind I was never going to forget them.

Just as I passed by a large crack in the pavement, I stopped. Someone had drawn a small troll peeking out of a drawn hole in the ground. The dark green weed that was growing out of the crack had been used as the hair.

The troll made me smile.

Some people had such incredible talent.

I pulled my phone from my pocket and snapped a picture. I paused, hooking my elbow around the handle of the shopping cart and scrolling until I pulled up my social media account.

Saw this little guy today. Was having a hard day, but this made me smile.

I posted the picture and then slipped my phone back into my pocket. If he made me smile, maybe someone else needed that too.

Blake was watching me as I pulled the cart up next to the trunk. His frown was pronounced as he studied me.

I shrugged. "What?" I asked as I felt for the trunk release.

"What were you doing?"

I pinched my lips closed as I moved to pack the groceries into the trunk. "Nothing."

"Do you normally take pictures of the ground?"

I glanced over my shoulder in the direction of the troll. I thought about telling Blake about it but figured he wouldn't care. "So? Maybe I like the ground."

Blake straightened and craned his neck as if he were trying to see what I had been looking at. "I doubt that," he said as he started moving toward the drawing.

"It's nothing. Can we go?" I asked as I quickly loaded the last few bags into the trunk and slammed it closed.

Blake glanced over at me. He looked skeptical as he studied me but then sighed and threw his keys into the air. "Yeah, sure."

The ride back to the house was quiet. Blake kept his wrist on the steering wheel and leaned toward the door as he drove. He didn't seem like he wanted to talk, so I kept my gaze forward.

When he pulled into the driveway, I got out before he could beat me to it. We both met up at the trunk. He had already strung quite a bit of bags over his arms when I leaned in to take one out.

"I've got this," he said, giving me a wink.

Not sure how to take that gesture, I decided to just ignore it and move to carry something. "It's okay. I can do this. You probably want to go home."

Blake paused but didn't move to let me take them. Instead, he continued until he had all the bags, and I was left carrying a gallon of milk.

"I don't mind." He shrugged as he wiggled a hand free to shut the trunk. "Besides, I don't really have any place to be."

"Really?" I asked as I followed after him. "Your parents don't want you home?"

After Mom's diagnosis, I couldn't imagine being any place but with her. My friends took a back seat to movie nights and popcorn as we snuggled in her bed.

Blake paused, glancing over his shoulder. "Naw. They won't miss me."

Before I could respond, the front door opened, and Mom filled the door frame. She clapped her hands and stepped to the side as she waved Blake in. I could hear her exclamations of joy as Blake carried in the groceries. You would think the man had discovered the cure to her cancer with the way she was going on.

But that was Mom, and more so now that she was sick. Every task—no matter how mundane—was a chance to celebrate.

I guess I couldn't blame her. Life was short and precious, and I loved that my mom chose to focus on every aspect of the human experience.

"You're such a sweet daughter," Mom said as I walked into the kitchen to deposit my groceries. Her arm wrapped around my shoulders, and I was suddenly pulled next to her. "Dad will be so glad that he didn't have to brave the aisles." She planted a kiss on my cheek.

My heart surged with affection, but I wiggled from her grasp. Mom had been adamant that she didn't want things to change once she was diagnosed. I'd even heard her crying to Dad a few months before we moved that she feared her children wouldn't get the chance to be teenagers like everyone else.

That made me realize that to make my mother happy, there were times I needed to shrink from her affection. Or act sullen like a teenager. When I did, her smile only grew bigger.

"Ma, please," I said as I set the bags on the counter and pretended to wipe away her kiss.

She gave me a sheepish smile. "Sorry. Habit." Her gaze

landed on Blake who had filled up a cup of water and was standing next to the sink while he drank it. "Thanks for taking our Susie to the grocery store. It would have been nice for her own brother to take her"—Mom waved her hand in the direction of Paul's room—"but you know how teenage boys are."

I wanted to say that Paul faked the teenage angst to make Mom happy, but I doubted it. He was determined to be as distant as he could from our family. I'd heard "coping mechanism" thrown around a lot between doctors and nurses, but it still irritated me.

He didn't know how long we had with Mom. He should be soaking in as much time as he could.

"I'll put these away while you go sit and rest," I said as I took the egg carton that Mom had just removed from the plastic bag.

She scoffed, but I put my hand firmly on her back and began pushing her from the kitchen. I could feel her desire to fight me, but then she sighed and nodded. "Fine. But once you're done, don't go disappear. And don't forget about me out here."

I nodded, and she shuffled over to the couch and sat down on it.

Blake and I spent the next ten minutes trying to figure out where to put the groceries. I wanted them to be somewhere that would be easy for Mom to grab. Once they were all put away, I glanced over at Blake.

He looked completely at home as he leaned against the

counter with his arms folded. He glanced up at me and smiled when he caught me studying him.

Heat raced to my cheeks, and I cleared my throat.

"So, what's the plan for the rest of the day?"

I blinked. I really hadn't thought that far ahead. "I dunno. Eat and watch TV."

He glanced around and nodded. "Sounds like my kind of evening."

3

SUSIE

When Blake said he had no interest in going home...he meant it.

He stayed at our house until Dad got home. He got invited to eat dinner with us. And he even stayed to help with clean up. I'd never seen so much of one of my brother's friends. Ever.

In New York, Paul was always leaving to go to someone else's house. We barely even saw him let alone knew who his friends were. So having both guys in the house this much was...unsettling.

Especially since I was growing to like Blake's laugh and the way he teased my mom. He looked so at home here that it made me wonder what was so bad about his actual home life to make him want to stay here as much as he was.

My thoughts were whirling around in my mind when

Mom stood up from the table she was sitting at and moved to the fridge to pull out the ice cream I'd purchased earlier. She wiggled her eyebrows as she pointed toward it. "Anyone want dessert?"

I nodded at the same time Blake whooped in agreement. Paul was too distracted on his phone to comment, and Dad looked like he was ready to keel over from exhaustion. Mom gave him a sympathetic smile and told him to go lay down. She then turned her attention to Blake and I. "Spoons. Bowls," she said as she pointed to Blake and then to me.

I gave her a salute and hurried to retrieve my assignment. Blake beat me back to Mom, but it was only because the spoons were closer to where she stood. When I set the bowls next to the spoons, he nudged my shoulder with his.

"Better luck next time, kiddo," he said.

I dropped my jaw. "It's only because you had the advantage of being closer. I had double the distance to cover."

He shrugged and then sucked in his breath. "That sounds like something the loser would say."

I narrowed my eyes at him. "Name the place and time, and I will whoop you." I ended my statement with a punch to his arm...which did nothing. I doubted I even dented his skin. There were sheer muscles under his shirt, and it almost made me want to take back my challenge, but I didn't.

After all, it wasn't like I was that serious or anything.

Mom chuckled, and we both turned to look at her. She was busily scooping ice cream and smiling like she'd just heard the best joke.

"What?" I asked as I leaned forward and snatched a small scoop of the moose tracks ice cream that she'd just put in.

She shook her head as she swatted my hand away—but I was too fast and dropped the ice cream into my mouth. "Nothing," she said.

I narrowed my eyes. "That smile does not mean nothing."

Mom paused before she looked up and then turned her attention to Blake and then back to me. "It's just that, if I didn't know better, I would say you two are dating."

I'd chosen that time to chew my ice cream and just as Mom's words met my ears, I swallowed. Hard. I winced as the half-chewed chocolate scraped my throat as it went down. But I needed to stop her from saying anything else, so I managed out a "What?" in my raspy voice.

Mom didn't seem to pick up on my desperation that she stop. Instead, she pointed her ice cream covered finger in my direction and then landed on Blake. "I would say you two are dating."

"Ma," I said, thankful that my mouth was empty so I could speak my clearly. "What are you talking about?"

She shrugged. "Is it out of the realm of possibilities?"

I peeked over at Blake who looked amused from this

conversation. When his gaze landed on me, I snapped my focus back on Mom. "Yes. Yes, it is."

"Why?"

My cheeks heated from Mom's question. What was I supposed to say to that? "Well—"

"That would be perfect."

Her sudden outburst startled Blake and me. We turned our attention to her, and as soon as I took in her mischievous smile, I knew we were in trouble.

"You two should pretend to date."

Yep. I knew it. Mom had officially gone crazy.

"I'm sorry, what? Mom, you're crazy," I hurried to say, hoping I could show Blake that I had no intention of going along with this before he stepped in and rejected me in a very real way.

Mom shook her head, clearly determined to make this a thing. "No, I'm not. You two could help each other out."

"We could?"

I glanced over at Blake, surprised that he wasn't running straight out of the house and far away from my family and our insane ideas.

"You want to get your ex back. What was her name—"

"Hannah."

"Hannah." Mom waved over at me. "Susie is new to school, and you could help show her around." Mom then clapped her hands. "It's the perfect solution."

Mom and I had watched too many Hallmark movies. I needed to remind her that this was real life. "I don't think

Blake wants to fake date me, ma," I said with a snort. I glanced over at him, fully expecting that he was going to go along with my response.

But he didn't. Instead, it looked as if he were mulling this idea over.

What was happening?

"I mean, it's not the worst idea." He shrugged as he glanced over at me. "Hannah would see what she's missing, and you would be free to use Glories Bluff's most eligible bachelor however you want."

My cheeks warmed at his words as all sorts of thoughts floated around in my mind. Thoughts that I shouldn't be having about Blake even if we decided to fake date each other.

"Paul, what do you think about all of this?" Surely, my brother would reject this idea. After all, Blake was his friend, not mine. If we were fake dating, when would my brother see him?

Paul glanced up from his phone. "Think about what?"

I sighed. Typical Paul. "Blake and I fake dating so he can get his girlfriend back."

Paul flicked his gaze from me, to Blake, and then back down to his phone. "If he wants to date you." He grew silent as he focused back on what he was doing.

I sighed. So much for family sticking together.

Mom had finished dishing up a bowl and slid it over to Blake who picked it up and then grabbed a spoon. I half expected him to start inhaling the food, but to my surprise, he started walking toward me.

He lifted my hand and set the bowl inside of my palm. Then he smiled at me. "This is just a preview of what you are going to get if you agree to fake date Blake Marshall."

I swallowed, feeling myself drowning in his bright blue eyes and half smile. It wasn't fair that he was inches from me and smelled like the outdoors. How was a girl supposed to say no to this?

"Promise?" I managed out before I could stop myself from speaking.

He raised an eyebrow. "Promise what?"

I swallowed, forcing my confidence to the surface. "Promise that I'll get the royal treatment?" If I was going to go along with this game, I was going to get something out of it besides making Mom happy, which I could tell that our little exchange was doing from her wide smile I could make out from the corner of my eye.

Blake studied me and then his half smile grew into a full smile. His teeth were perfectly white and perfectly straight. I doubted that he had an imperfection anywhere on his body.

"Promise." He extended out his pinky.

I studied it and then met his gesture.

"Stamp it," he said as he moved to press his thumb against mine.

When we were done, he dropped his hand and turned

to Mom. "Mrs. Jordan, have I ever told you that you were a genius?"

He and Mom continued their conversation about how brilliant this idea was while they ate their ice cream. My ice cream melted in my bowl as my stomach flip flopped. I was no longer hungry. Instead, I was sitting at the table, stressing about what this meant for me.

For school.

Blake seemed confident that everything was going to be fine. And maybe he was right. After all, I'd only just moved here. I had yet to experience my first day of school. Maybe I was freaking out over nothing.

I peeked over at Blake who was laughing at something Mom had said. I allowed myself to study him for a moment before dropping my attention back to my ice cream soup.

They talked the rest of the evening, until Mom's eyes began to droop. I pushed my chair way from the table and scooped up my bowl and spoon and brought it over to the sink. "I think it's time to call it a night," I said as I pulled the dish towel that was hung over the oven handle and dried my hands.

Blake looked disappointed, but he seemed to pick up on Mom's exhaustion, so he nodded. "That's probably a good thing," he said as he pushed his chair out and stood. "If I stay here any longer, I'm going to turn into a pumpkin."

Mom moved to stand as well, but before she could,

Blake was there with his hands wrapped around the back of the chair as he helped her pull it out from under the table. She gave him a weak smile just before a yawn emerged. "Thanks, Blake." She moved to walk by him but then stopped and reached up to pat his cheek. "I'm glad we moved here. It'll be nice to see you more."

He grinned and then watched her walk away.

The sound of her bedroom door closing marked her departure and the start of my alone time with Blake. He really didn't move to leave, and I started to wonder if he was going to grab a pillow and a blanket and camp out here.

I busied myself with rinsing the dishes and loading them into the dishwasher. I opened the cabinet under the sink and then stopped. I'd forgotten to get some dishwashing soap.

"Dang it," I muttered under my breath as I shut the dishwasher door.

"Everything okay?"

I glanced over my shoulder to see Blake studying me. I blew out my breath. "Yeah. I just forgot dishwasher tabs when we went to Harts."

Blake crossed his arms as he studied me. Then he shrugged. "Well, as your new pseudo boyfriend, all you have to do is ask, and I'll get some for you."

My cheeks heated at the mention of our arrangement. I quickly shook my head. "About that. We don't…" I waved my hand in front of me as if that was all I needed to do to let him off the hook.

He just quirked an eyebrow.

I leaned forward. "We don't have to do this. Mom is just being...mom." I hated the idea of disappointing my mother but didn't want Blake to feel obligated to follow through with this plan.

"Are you chickening out already?" His smile sent shivers down my back.

The fact that he was so playful about this gave me hope that perhaps, he was okay with this plan. And that thought made me feel excited and uneasy at the same time.

"I'm not backing out. I'm just giving you the chance to change your mind."

"I stamped it, so I'm all in."

I swallowed. Was I really prepared to do this?

Blake must have sensed my hesitancy because in two swift steps, he was standing in front of me. He extended his hand and let his fingers linger about an inch in front of my arm. "Listen, I don't want to disappoint your mom, and I'm not going to lie. It would feel great to get Hannah back." He offered me a small smile. "I promise you will have the time of your life." Then he lifted his hands up. "No touching, and I will be a gentleman."

That might be the issue, but I didn't say that. Instead, I studied him, wishing I could feel platonic toward him. I wanted to agree, fake date to make mom happy, and walk away unscathed. Which was still an option if I could only get my feelings to settle.

The strength to oppose him left my body, so I just nodded. "Okay."

His expression lightened. "Okay?"

I nodded again. "I'll be your fake girlfriend."

He cheered and clapped his hands. "Perfect. Oh, this is going to be epic." He clapped his hand on my shoulder. "You won't regret this."

I watched him as he pumped his fist in the air and walked through the kitchen and out to the hallway. In a matter of seconds, I was completely alone.

I blew out my breath as I collapsed against the counter, his words repeating in my mind.

You won't regret this.

And I hoped he was right.

Problem was, there was a small part of me. Way back in the depth of my mind that knew the truth.

I would regret this.

It was only a matter of how much.

4

SUSIE

Blake was taking his duty as my fake boyfriend seriously.

I was standing out on our wrap around porch Monday morning, waiting for him to pick me up. I tried to convince him that I would be okay. That I really just wanted to hitch a ride with Dad on his way into town, but Blake wasn't having any of it.

He called me Sunday night to make sure that I would be ready the next day, and when I woke up, I discovered a text that he sent me that consisted of a clock and smiley emoji.

The boy was persistent.

I glanced down at my graphic tee and ripped jeans, debating if I should go back inside and change. I wasn't sure who I wanted to be at this new school. From what I'd seen around town, cowboy boots and plaid button up shirts seemed to be the town's style.

If I wanted an uneventful high school experience, maybe fitting in was the way to go.

I tipped the toes of my Converses together and sighed. Problem was, I didn't have those items and I doubted Blake would want to stop by the local Tractor Supply to load me up.

If I was going to be different, I might as well lean into it.

The crunching sound of gravel on the wheels of a truck drew my attention up. I squinted through the morning sun to see Blake sitting in the driver's seat. The glare of the light made it hard to make out features, but when he raised his fingers off the steering wheel, I responded with a wave.

"He's saying hi to me, dork," Paul said. He shouldered me as he walked past.

The force of his nudge sent me forward a step. I glared at him, but he didn't seem to notice as he bounded down the front steps and over to Blake's truck. I thought about retaliating—or at least using a strongly worded come back—but he was climbing into the passenger seat before I could respond.

So, I sighed and made my way to the truck. When I pulled open the small side door, music blared from the speakers. Paul was jamming out to the beat while Blake shot me an apologetic smile.

"Morning," he said.

I just nodded as I climbed in and slammed the door shut behind me. I buckled while Blake reversed his truck and pulled onto the main highway. I kept my gaze out the window as he drove past fields and fields of cows and sheep.

"Ready for today?" Blake's voice barely made it over Paul's music, and I had to lean forward just to make sure I heard what he said.

"What?" I asked.

"Ready for today?" he asked again, this time louder.

I nodded and settled back in my seat. I crossed my arms and kept my focus anywhere but the rearview mirror where every few moments, Blake glanced back at me.

Whatever he was doing, I wasn't having any of this. Even if he was going to take fake dating seriously, that didn't mean we had to pretend when others weren't around. As far as I was concerned, we were a couple at school and school alone. Anywhere else, he was my brother's best friend, and I was the geeky younger sister.

This was how I was going to maintain my sanity...and protect my heart from whatever consequence could come of this decision.

Thankfully, Blake eventually stopped trying to catch my gaze. He focused his attention forward, and he and Paul made as much small chat as they could through the blaring music.

By the time Blake pulled into the school parking lot, I

was ready to get out. I needed to define myself as someone other than Paul's sister and Blake's...whatever I was. I needed friends that matched who I was.

As soon as the car stopped and the engine was turned off, I pulled open the door and hopped out. A row of trucks ran the length of the parking lot, and I snorted. There was no way I would have seen one of these gas guzzlers in New York. All the pretentious residents' heads would spin if they saw the sight that unfolded in front of me.

And I was okay with that. I didn't fit in there—I was too plain for them. Perhaps, here, I could redefine myself.

The sound of the doors shutting behind me caused me to quicken my pace through the parked cars. I could hear Blake and Paul carrying on a conversation behind me, and I wasn't sure what the topic would turn to if they caught up with me, so I kept a healthy pace in front of them.

I pulled open the large, glass exterior door and welcomed the blast of cool air that surrounded me. The heat outside, mixed with the sprint I had to maintain to keep ahead, left me panting and sweating. Which is such a great combination on one's first day of school...

Not.

I sighed as I pulled out my schedule from my backpack and scanned down until I saw my locker number. Hoping I'd get there with as little mishaps as possible, I stuck to the wall as I made my way down the hallway.

Just as I rounded the corner, I felt the weight of an arm

landing on my shoulders. I stopped, frozen in place as I turned slowly, my heart pounding.

"Where are you off to so fast?" Blake's low, flirting tone caused my heart to race.

I glanced up to see him smiling down at me. His eyebrows were raised, and I wondered if he really cared about where I was going or if he was just pretending.

Then I shook my head. Of course, he was pretending. He was talking to me to get his ex back. That was all.

I cleared my throat and took a step to the side, hoping that would break his contact with me. It didn't. He just stretched with me, keeping his arm on my shoulders.

I sighed, realizing that he was here to stay. I might as well stop trying to fight it. "I'm looking for my locker," I said as I held up my schedule.

That seemed to do the trick. Blake dropped his arm, so he could take the paper from me. "Well, you're headed in the wrong direction. Locker bay E is that way." He pointed in the direction we'd just come.

I nodded and turned to follow his directions. Just as I walked away, a hand slipped into mine. Our fingers entwined, and once again, I was stopped dead in my tracks. I glanced up to see Blake's smile had faded, and he was staring straight ahead.

"I—"

"Hannah's walking toward us right now," he whispered as he flicked his gaze down to meet mine.

The desperation and pain that existed there was

enough to cause my heart to ache for him. Even though my initial reaction was to pull my hand away, I didn't. Instead, I tightened my grip on him as I glanced around, hoping to catch a glimpse of *Hannah*.

I didn't have to look far. Every teen movie I'd ever seen depicted the girl in front of me down to a science. She was tall, blonde, and curvy. She was flanked by girls, and when she walked, the sea of students parted around her. She was wearing a miniskirt and heels with a small purse hanging from her shoulder.

No backpack. No schoolbooks. It was as if she were at the mall, not the hallway of learning.

I peeked up at Blake who seemed to be trying hard not to look her direction. This was the girl he liked? This was the girl he'd been dating? Why was I worried about something starting between us? I was a fool to be concerned. Especially since *this* was his idea of a perfect girl.

I suddenly wanted to hide.

But I promised to help Blake, so I would. I turned and faced him, letting out the loudest and most obnoxious laugh I could. It hurt my ears, but if it got Hannah's attention, it would be worth it.

"Oh, my gosh. You're so funny," I said as I stepped closer to Blake, tightening my grip on his hand and smacking him in the chest with my other one.

Blake looked startled as he stared down at me. "What are you doing?" he hissed.

"Just go with it." Then I laughed again. "That's the girl that you dumped?" Then I twirled my finger around on his chest which only caused Blake's eyebrows to rise. But I didn't stop there. I leaned in closer, smelling his cologne and feeling as if this was the worst idea ever. "Well, it's my gain," I managed to get out as I tipped my gaze up to meet his and suddenly became very aware of how close our lips were to each other.

From the corner of my eye, I could see the crowd around us slow. I wasn't sure if Hannah was still around, but we were certainly drawing the attention of the other students.

I stood next to Blake, waiting for him to do something. If he didn't move or touch me, this wasn't going to work out. Just when I thought he was going to call the entire charade off, his free arm wrapped around my waist, and I was suddenly being pulled against him.

My free hand flew up to his chest, so I could brace myself. My body collided with his as he dropped our clasped hands and pushed me toward the wall behind me. He caged me in as he stared down at me.

My breath slowed as I stared up at him. His warmth cascaded over me as we stood there, our gazes locked on each other. I couldn't help myself as I glanced down at his lips and then dragged my gaze back up to meet his once more.

"Wha—what are you doing?" I finally breathed out.

He furrowed his brow as he studied me. "Giving them a show." He frowned. "Like you."

Right. Show. Fake.

I had to repeat those words a few times in my head to clear the fog that I felt from being this close to Blake. I blinked in an effort to ground myself. I peered over his shoulder just as the first bell rang.

The small crowd that had started to form dispersed. I expected Blake to pull away at the sound, but to my surprise, he didn't. Instead, he remained, caging me in between the wall and his body.

I glanced back up at him, wondering why he was still standing here when it was obvious that Hannah was no longer around, and it was almost as if he were wondering that too. His gaze was soft, and it was as if he were frozen in place.

When it became obvious that he wasn't going to move on his own, I cleared my throat. "I think we made our point," I said as I patted his arm.

He startled and pulled back. He pushed the hand that had been resting on the wall behind me through his hair as his expression turned sheepish. "Sorry," he murmured.

I shrugged as I hoisted my backpack higher up on my shoulder. "It's no big deal. It was our first go at this whole faking a relationship thing. It was bound to have some hiccups." I gave him a weak smile.

He nodded. "True. We'll get it figured out and, next time, she won't know what hit her."

Bleh.

Hannah.

Why did I hate it when he talked about her? It was like vomit to my ears.

"I should get going," I said quickly, the desire to take off down the hallway overcoming me.

Blake nodded. "Yeah. Me too. I have to make it across campus before the last bell rings."

I decided to focus my attention on my schedule. "And I have to figure out where I'm going. I've got chemistry."

Blake suddenly appeared next to me as he studied my schedule as well. He then straightened and pointed to the left. "Go out the door at the end of the hall and cross the courtyard. Room 65 is just inside the science building."

Grateful for his help and wanting to distance myself from him, I nodded and took a few steps forward.

"We have lunch together."

I stopped and turned. "What?"

Blake motioned toward my schedule. "We have lunch together. We should sit at the same table." He hooked his thumb around his backpack strap. "Wanna meet me at the big picture windows, and then we can get our food together?"

He looked so...innocent, standing there, asking me to eat lunch with him. I wanted to desperately believe that he was asking me to sit with him because he wanted me to, but I had a sinking suspicion that Hannah had her lunch period with us.

5

SUSIE

I walked into English class and scanned the room for a place to sit. So far, period one and two had been uneventful. The teachers had packets of homework for me to do, and the students seemed friendly enough.

I was rapidly learning that Glories Bluff High didn't get a lot of new move ins. I was an anomaly, and from the glances and whispers my direction, people were intrigued by who I was and why I would choose to move to Montana over living in New York. I told them about Dad's job and left it there.

I really wasn't ready to start spilling the beans about Mom just yet.

I spotted a seat in the back, so I made a beeline for it. I dropped into my seat, letting my backpack slip off my shoulder and fall to the ground next to me. I was leaning over to open my backpack when I heard a voice next to me.

"So, you're the new girl I've heard so much about."

I glanced up to see a pair of bright blue eyes and a cocky half smile. His hair was dark brown and hung just above his eyebrows. He gave me a wink as he settled back in his seat and raked his gaze over me.

Not sure what to do, I just smiled. "Yep," I said as I pulled out my notebook and pencil and set it on my desk in front of me.

He put his weight on his elbow as he leaned closer to me. "Stetson," he said.

Was that his name or some Montana greeting? My cheeks heated. Why was he even paying attention to me? My whole goal here was to become invisible, and I was failing horribly at that.

"This is where you tell me your name." His tone was deep, and even though I was oblivious to a lot, I knew what he was trying to do.

"Susie."

"Oh, Harold, keep it in your pants."

I turned to see a girl with a baggy sweatshirt, ponytail, and jeans shoot daggers in Stetson/Harold's direction.

"His name is Harold. His last name *is* Stetson, but his first name is *Harold*." She sounded out every letter, and that just made me smile.

"You're such a killjoy, *Patricia*," Stetson said as he

turned around and started chatting with the guy next to him.

Patricia stuck her tongue out at him and then turned to me. "You can call my Patty."

"Susie."

She smiled. "Looks like we were both named from the seventies."

I nodded. "Named after my grandmother."

"Great grandmother."

We chuckled.

"So, you moved here from New York?"

I blew out my breath. "News travels fast around here."

She shrugged. "Perks of a small town. Nothing stays a secret for long."

I wasn't sure if that was a good thing or bad thing.

Patty seemed to pick up on my hesitancy. "Other than that, Glories Bluff is great. I've lived here my whole life."

"Good to know."

Just then, the teacher, Mr. Borden, walked in and started the class. I wanted to talk more to Patty, but Mr. Borden wasn't one to let up once he got started. It wasn't until he separated us into groups to discuss an Edgar Allen Poe poem, that I was able to talk to Patty again.

In between analyzing meaning, we chatted about things we liked. Surprisingly, we had a lot in common. We both loved music and soccer. She was on the school's team, and we made plans to talk to the coach to see if I could try out.

When the bell rang and we gathered our things, she waited for me to walk out with her.

"Going to lunch?" she asked as she adjusted her backpack strap on her shoulder.

I nodded, butterflies assaulting my stomach when the plans that I'd made with Blake surfaced. I was supposed to meet him, and we were supposed to eat together. All in the hopes that Hannah would see and suddenly want to take him back.

My fake dating plan with Blake wasn't really something I wanted to share with Patty, yet keeping it a secret felt like a betrayal of our newly formed relationship. If secrets really do travel fast in a small town, how long would it take for Blake's and my arrangement to get out?

And what would that do to Blake?

"Yeah, you?"

She nodded. "That's perfect. We can eat together."

I gave her a weak smile. I wasn't sure how I was going to explain Blake to Patty, and I was secretly hoping that I wouldn't have to.

"I made plans to eat with my brother's best friend, if that's okay," tumbled from my mouth before I could stop it.

She quirked an eyebrow.

"That was before I had someone else to eat with." I winced as my words met my own lips. That just made me sound like a total loser.

"Oh, cool."

Patty left it at that. We made small talk as we walked from the arts building to the main building where the gym, office, and cafeteria was. As soon as we pulled open the side door that led into the cafeteria, Blake appeared. He wrapped me up into a hug, and my heart pounded. Not just from the close proximity, but the fact that I was fairly certain that Patty was confused.

I mean, I'd introduced him as my brother's best friend, not a guy who randomly hugged me.

"I was wondering when you were going to show up," he said once he pulled away. His smile was wide, and he gave me a wink as if we held a secret that no one else knew. I liked it...probably a bit too much.

"Sorry. Patty and I were walking a tad slow."

"Patty?"

I nodded in her direction, and Blake glanced over. His smile widened. "Aren't you Tommy's little sister?"

"Yep. And you're Blake Marshall." Patty folded her arms and narrowed her eyes.

Blake chuckled. "Yep. That's me."

Not sure what this stare down meant, I turned to focus on the lunchroom. Hannah wasn't hard to spot. She was sitting at the table surrounded by her minions. Call me crazy, but when her gaze met mine, I could literally feel the daggers she was sending my direction.

Not sure what to do, I gave her a quick smile and then turned my focus back on Blake and Patty. There was a strange interaction going on between them, and it was making me uncomfortable.

"Let's go get some food," I said, even though my stomach was so knotted that I doubted I would be able to eat anything.

Thankfully, Blake and Patty didn't argue with me. Instead, we walked over to the entrance of the kitchen and just as I moved to grab a tray, Blake beat me to it.

"Here, let me get that for you," he said, his arm brushing mine.

Tingles erupted across my skin, freezing me in place. Before I could stop him, he had a tray in each hand and was heading to the first section of food.

"I can do it," I said as I moved to grab my tray back.

Blake glanced down. He looked confused as he studied me. "It's okay. I can do it." He leaned forward and whispered, "Royal treatment."

My cheeks heated, and I wanted to go along with it, but I also didn't want to run off my new friend. From the way she was staring at Blake and I, she was thoroughly confused. I wanted Hannah to think Blake and I were dating, but that was the last thing I wanted Patty to think. Especially after her cool reaction to him.

It was a mess, but I was determined to do some prevention before it spiraled out of control. It was my first day of school, yet I felt as if I was ruining it all.

I wanted things to be different here. I wanted things to

be easier. I was already dealing with a life altering issue, and I didn't have room to add anymore drama.

Plus, no matter how I felt about Blake, this was all fake to him. He was determined to get Hannah, and at the end of this whole charade, I was going to be alone. At least with Patty, I had a friend, and when Mom got worse or Blake got all lovey-dovey with Hannah, I was going to need that support system.

No need to foster a relationship with a boy who seems determined to end up with another girl.

But I also had to stop Blake from picking up the soggy looking sandwich that he was currently eyeing. I hurried to catch up with him and placed my hand on his wrist before he dropped the sandwich on my tray.

He glanced up at me, and suddenly, I realized how close we were. His gaze met mine, and for a moment, everything around me stilled. All I could focus on was Blake and…I hated that.

"No sandwich," I said when I finally found my voice.

He quirked an eyebrow. "No?"

I shook my head. "No."

He dropped the sandwich back into the cooler and glanced around. "Then what do you eat?"

He followed behind me as I moved through the cafeteria. I picked up an apple, yogurt, and granola bar, and set them on the extended tray. I ended with a small bowl of soup with crackers and turned to smile at Blake.

"That's it?"

I nodded. "That'll do."

He shrugged as he handed over my tray. "Hold tight. I'll grab what I want and then pay."

Heat pricked the back of my neck from his words. He was paying? Why? I knew he was a nice guy. I just didn't know he was this kind of gentleman. "It's okay—" I started before I realized he'd already taken off.

I sighed as I shuffled over to the wall and waited. When my gaze met Patty's, I straightened and smiled. She looked hesitant before she shook her head slightly and headed my direction.

She had what looked like spaghetti and a small piece of garlic bread on her plate. "Good choices," she said as she nodded toward my tray.

I shrugged. "I think I'll be bringing food from now on. But we didn't really have anything that would keep, so I'll go shopping tonight."

"Pains of moving."

I blew out my breath. "Yep."

She glanced around and then back to me. "Ready to pay?"

I peeked in Blake's direction, and an internal struggle boiled up. Was he going to be angry? Probably not. He was just being kind and thought this was what he needed to do. If anything, it was probably better that I pay, just to make sure we had some boundaries set. I didn't want to owe him anything.

"Yep," I said as I turned and headed toward the

cashier. I hated that I felt guilty for leaving Blake after he asked me to stay, but my reasoning helped me to keep my focus on the cashier as I paid.

I waited for Patty to scan her card, and we headed out into the lunchroom. As soon as I stepped out into the throng of tables, I felt Hannah's gaze on me. I peeked in her direction to see her stare at me for a moment before her gaze fell behind me.

She was not even trying to hide the fact that she was looking for Blake. I thought about waiting around for Blake to finish but then pushed that out. Even if we were fake boyfriend and girlfriend, that didn't mean we had to be next to each other all the time.

Right?

"I usually sit over by the windows," Patty said as she nodded in the direction of the huge picture windows along the far wall.

"Yeah?" I asked as I followed behind her.

When we got to the far corner table, we both set our trays down and pulled out our chairs. I was in the midst of opening my yogurt when Blake's voice startled me. I yanked the lid the rest of the way off, splattering yogurt everywhere.

"You left me," he said, the clattering of his tray muffling his words.

I grabbed a napkin out of the dispenser in the middle of the table and began wiping up the mess I'd just made. "Sorry. Patty wanted to make sure we got this table."

"Oh really?" Blake glanced over at Patty who was busy twirling her spaghetti on her fork.

When she didn't say anything, Blake glanced over at me.

"I thought I was going to pay for you," he said as he nudged me with his shoulder.

I shrugged. "It's okay. I prefer to pay for myself."

He was quiet for a moment before he started to dig into his food. He'd picked up a few sandwiches and bags of chips. It looked like it could feed a small army.

"Hungry?" I asked.

He shrugged as his one bite demolished half the sandwich. "This is what it takes to be the football team's best player." He smiled at me as he chewed.

Right. He was a football player. I couldn't remember exactly what position he played, and when I ran through the positions I knew and got to tight end, I stopped thinking.

Instead, I focused on eating what was left of my yogurt.

Silence engulfed our table as we all sat chewing. Patty looked uncomfortable, and Blake looked relaxed as he leaned back in his chair. I caught his gaze wandering over to Hannah a few times which caused my own gaze to follow in the same direction.

One of the times, Hannah turned her attention to me, and I pulled my gaze back to my lunch in front of me, heat penetrating my cheeks. What was I doing? Why did I even care if Blake was looking in the same direction that his ex-girlfriend was sitting in? The whole point of this was to make her jealous.

And from her pinched lips and death stare, our plan was working.

"I gotta go meet with my counselor," Patty said as she gathered her trash onto her tray and stood.

"Really?" I asked, moving to stand and then realizing that I still had my soup to eat. Eating soup and walking down high school hallways wasn't a good combination.

"It's okay. We can connect after school?" It was obvious that Patty had no intention of including Blake as her gaze focused directly on me.

I parted my lips. I wanted to say yes, but I also needed to get home. "I have something after school, but maybe after dinner?" By then, Mom would be in bed, and I would be bored. It would be nice to have a little distraction.

Patty grinned. "Perfect."

I waved at her as she took off down the hallway and disappeared round the corner. I sighed as I turned my attention back to my rapidly cooling soup.

"Am I your plans after school?" Blake asked, the tone of his voice taking on a flirty hint.

I glanced over at him, feeling completely confused. What exactly were we doing here? If this was all fake, why did he make it feel real sometimes? I wasn't sure *exactly* how fake relationships worked, but I was fairly certain that flirting wasn't part of those rules.

So, I took a drink from my water bottle and shook my head. "I have a hot date..." I paused, just to see his reaction.

His eyebrows rose slightly, and it made my heart pick up speed. He was interested in what I was doing, that was for sure.

Not wanting to get lost in my own head, I quickly finished. "...with my mom."

He relaxed a bit as he slumped against his chair. "You had me going, little Susie," he said as he opened one of his chip bags more and then tipped his head back and allowed the remaining crumbs to slide into his mouth. "You had me thinking that you'd already found your Prince Charming here at Glories Bluff and our pact was off."

I scoffed before I'd even realized that I made noise. Feeling embarrassed, I glanced over to see Blake studying me. Heat permeated my cheeks as I fiddled with my tray. "I doubt that I've caught the eye of any guy here," I said so softly that I feared he hadn't heard and was going to ask me what I'd said.

"Are you joking?"

I glanced up, confused by his reaction. "What?"

He leaned forward, resting his elbows on his knees which brought his face dangerously close to mine. "I saw Sawyer, the captain of the soccer team looking at you." He flexed his hand. "I was ready to gouge his eyes out."

My face was officially on fire. I swallowed, the heat from my skin drying out my throat. No amount of spit seemed to help. "What?" I mumbled, hoping he'd confess that his words were all a joke made to make me feel self-conscious. That I was really a nobody that people never paid attention to.

At least then, I could agree with him.

He shrugged. "You're beautiful. You have to know that."

My ears were ringing now. Did he just say beautiful? "I am?"

He met my gaze and held it for a moment. Then he reached forward, and I felt my breath catch in my throat. Was he going to make a move? How did I feel about that?

Then his hand landed on the top of my head, and he tousled it. His smile broke out across his face as he leaned in. "For my best friend's little sis, you're adorable."

I stared at him as he tossed his garbage onto his tray and moved to stand. Then he winked at me, bent down, and brushed his lips against my cheek. Just as he started to pull away, he stopped for a moment to whisper, "I think she took the bait. Hook, line, and sinker."

Then he disappeared.

I sat there, stunned, as I watched him walk through the cafeteria, dump his garbage in a nearby trash, and disappear.

When my heart finally settled and my skin returned to room temperature, I stood.

One thing was for sure; Blake and I needed to set

boundaries. If we were going to fake this relationship, he was going to have to keep his distance.

The longer I spent with Blake, the faster I was beginning to realize that if I didn't get my crap together soon, it was going to be too late.

He was going to have me snatched.

Hook, line, and sinker.

6

SUSIE

Paul barely pressed on the brakes when he pulled into the driveway after school, leaving me to roll out of the car like they teach people to do when disembarking a moving train. Tuck and roll, baby. Tuck and roll.

Apparently, he was meeting Blake and some friends at a diner in town, and I was his nuisance of a sister that was creeping in on his social life.

I mean, I was happy for my brother that he was finding friends and a new life his senior year of high school, but I didn't appreciate the new streaks of grass I was sporting on my jeans.

I grumbled as I stood, brushing my knees off.

Whatever had Paul so cranky was making life with him a pain.

"Jerk," I mumbled under my breath as I reached down

to grab my backpack. Maybe if I showed Mom and Dad what Paul had done to me, I could convince them to buy me a car...maybe.

I sighed as I laughed at my own joke.

Of course, Mom and Dad weren't going to buy me a car. They were convinced that Paul and I would grow closer together if we had to share a car. They worried that with Mom's cancer, we'd grow apart. And they were sort of right on that. But I still loved my brother, and I knew he loved me. We just had vastly different opinions on things that mattered.

For me, it was non-grass-stained pants, and for him, it was making small talk with people he didn't know over malts and overly salted french fries.

Neither were wrong, but Paul was older, and let's face it, bigger. What he wanted, he got.

Not wanting to stand in the driveway, obsessing about my brother's newfound attitude or driving technique, I headed inside the house.

Mom was sitting at the bar, flipping through her recipe book. The one she put together with Nana Rogers before she passed away.

If that book was out, it meant Mom was feeling better. Which caused a warm fire to turn to embers in my gut. I missed my mom, and after the confusing day I had at school, I was ready to unload on her.

"Good afternoon, my sweet." Her smile was wide, and

even though I could tell that she was carrying a level of exhaustion around with her at all times, her beautiful soul shone through.

I dropped my backpack on the counter and moved in to kiss her on the cheek. Then I pulled back and read the page that she was on. "Strawberry and rhubarb pie?" I asked, my mouth watering at those words. If it was Nana Rogers' recipe, it was going to be exquisite.

Mom nodded. "I got a hankering for it this morning. I figured we could make it."

I squeezed her shoulders. "Of course." With Mom's chemo treatments, she'd gotten quite thin. Her once full face had disappeared, and I was beginning to see her bones become more and more defined.

It was heart wrenching. So, if she wanted food, I was going to make it with her and watch with glee as she devoured every bite.

It took me a hot minute to dig through the boxes that littered the house to find the mixing bowl, measuring spoons, and our matching aprons, but eventually, everything we needed to make this award-winning pie was laid out perfectly in front of us.

We started scooping the ingredients and laughing as we worked. Soon, the smell of simmering rhubarb and strawberries filled the house. It reminded me so much of my mom that it made my heart ache. I knew that I had her here. She was still alive. But the thought of losing her was always lingering in the back of my mind, and it was beginning to overshadow the memories I was currently making.

Which only made me feel like a horrible person. But how does one enjoy the time with a loved one when they realize that it's fleeting? How can I allow myself to be happy when I know how I'll feel in six months? In a year?

Life can change so quickly, and as much as I don't want to miss anything, I know that eventually, I won't have this.

Those thoughts were becoming a dark cloud above the moments with Mom.

"Does it not taste good?"

Mom's voice startled me. I was too wrapped up in my own thoughts while I stirred the pie filling to realize that I was staring hard at the backsplash in front of me. Glancing over, I saw Mom peering up at me.

I shook my head slightly, knowing that Mom couldn't read my thoughts, but just in case, I was going to push them from my mind. "Sorry. Long day."

Mom narrowed her eyes. I could tell that she didn't believe me, and I wondered if she was going to let it go. When the familiar, mischievous look hinted in her gaze, I knew I'd just said the wrong thing.

"Your aura is telling me everything," she said as she stuck a spoon into the mixture and pulled out a scoop. After taking a taste and then reaching over for a bit more sugar, she focused her attention on me. "Tonight is a full moon."

I knew where this was going. "Really, Ma?"

"Moon bathed water is the best for a confused mind." She waggled a finger in my direction as she moved to place the spoon into the sink.

I loved my mom and all of her quirks, but I was fairly certain drinking water that had been sitting out all night with a crystal in it wasn't going to do much to solve my issues—but then again, I was desperate. Maybe it would help me feel more grounded.

"It'll help you feel more grounded," Mom said a moment later.

I narrowed my eyes at her. Could she read my mind? I paused. She couldn't. Could she?

What was wrong with me? Of course, my mother didn't have superpowers to read my mind.

"I like to call it a superpower." She was busy rolling out the now chilled pie crust onto a butcher block.

Okay, this was now getting creepy.

I focused my attention on her. *Give Susie a million dollars.*

If she could read my mind, I was fairly certain she would balk at that. But instead of repeating what I'd channeled her direction, she hummed to herself as she flattened out the bumps in the crust.

I sighed just as the timer on the filling rang. Straightening, I clicked off the burner and moved the pot to the corner.

"Is it ready?" Mom sang out.

I nodded. "Looks delicious enough to eat."

"Don't do that," she said, whipping her gaze to me.

I just stood there with a grin on my face. When I was six, Mom had been making this exact pie, and I'd decided that I wanted some. When she left the kitchen, I confiscated the pot and was found in the nearby closet stuffing my face. It had become a family joke ever since then.

Mom reached for the nearby dishtowel and swatted me with it. I feigned pain as I moved to the oven to check if it was heated. We worked together, setting the pie crust into the dish and then pouring in the cooling filling. I rolled out the remaining dough, and then Mom went through and cut the strips for the lattice to lay on top.

Once the pie was in the oven, I glanced over at Mom to see that she looked tired. Her earlier cheery demeanor had slipped, and she looked like she needed a nap.

"You okay, Ma?" I asked as I moved toward her.

She let out a yawn but nodded. "I'm fine."

I shook my head. "Let's go start a movie so you can relax." I expected Mom to put up a fight, but she didn't. Instead, she let me lead her over into the living room where I pressed on her shoulders to indicate that she was going to sit.

I busied myself tucking a blanket around her and propping her head up with a pillow while she scrolled through the many already watched movies in our queue. When she landed on the newest Pride and Prejudice, I didn't put up a fight.

If Mom wanted to watch it, I would watch it.

"I'll pop some popcorn," I said after I finished tucking her feet in the blanket.

She nodded.

A sharp pain seized my gut when she didn't fight me about not spoiling my appetite for dinner. Mom had always been so strict with us growing up, and to see her wave it off like it was nothing only indicated to me that things were officially changing. And not for the good.

When I brought it up to Dad once, he waved me off telling me that we were older now. That they didn't expect us to follow the rules that they'd implemented when we were kids. I wanted to believe him, but I couldn't help but feel as if our family had given up.

I longed for the days when Mom and Dad yelled at us, kept us from watching TV, and limited eating sugary foods. Now, it seemed like we could do anything. And the fact that they gave us free reign only shone a spotlight on what we already knew.

That Mom was sick, and our lives would forever be changed because of that.

I sniffled as I watched the popcorn bag spinning in the microwave. The pie was in the oven, making the kitchen smell like heaven. I should be happy right now, but I wasn't. And I hated that.

With the popcorn bag in hand, I grabbed two waters from the fridge and brought them into the living room.

Once I got Mom situated with a bowl of popcorn and her water, I sat down next to her.

My phone chimed as the opening credits started. I slipped it from my pocket as I tossed a few popcorn pieces into my mouth.

Patty: Is now a good time to come over?

I peeked over at Mom. She had a soft smile on her lips as she watched Mrs. Bennett fluttering around the room in dismay.

"Are you okay with my new friend Patty coming over?" I asked. I didn't want people to look at my mom like she was sick, but I also knew that she wanted to be a part of my life. If it were up to me, I wouldn't go anywhere. Mom was my best friend, and I wanted to spend every moment I had with her.

Mom glanced over at me. "You found a friend?" Then she pinched her lips together. "I didn't mean to make that sound like I was surprised." She nodded. "Of course. I would love to meet all of your friends."

I texted Patty back with a thumbs up and our address. She replied with a: BRT and a smiley face emoji.

I set my phone down and grabbed another handful of popcorn. I didn't realize it, but Mom hadn't stopped staring at me. I quirked an eyebrow when I met her gaze. "What?" I asked through a mouthful of popcorn.

"Are you not going to tell me about this friend?"

"Patty?"

"Yes, Patty. At least I know her name now."

I took a sip of my water to wash down the popcorn that was sticking to my teeth. "She's in my English class, and we bonded over grandma sounding names." I ended my sentence with a pointed look in Mom's direction. She never had a good enough reason to name me Susan besides the fact that she —and I quote— "liked it."

I didn't find that to be a good enough reason to saddle your child with a name that sounded like it came with a walker with tennis balls.

"Oh, Susie," Mom said with a soft swat of my arm.

I giggled and buried further into the blankets and pillows that I had surrounded myself with. I leaned my head on her shoulder, and she rest her head on mine. It wasn't until I felt her shallow breathing that I realized that she'd fallen asleep. The sound and feeling calmed me.

So much so that I started to feel my eyelids droop closed. It wasn't until the doorbell startled me that I realized I'd fallen asleep. I ripped my eyelids open and sat up, glancing around to see if Mom had woken.

She was softly snoring with her head tipped back and her eyes closed. I tried to climb out from behind the pillows and blankets as quietly as I could, trying not to disturb her. It took some amazing ninja moves, but I succeeded. With my feet on the floor, I hurried over to the door before the bell was rung again.

When I opened the front door, I was met with Patty's smiling face. Our gazes met, and she held up a plastic bag in front of her.

"I come bearing gifts."

I smiled and hurried her into the house.

Patty paused, and I could tell that she was taking in a deep breath. "What is that smell?"

I took the bag from her and motioned her into the kitchen.

"Everything okay?" Patty asked as she glanced around the house.

I nodded as I pulled open the oven to check on the pie. Little bubbles were rising up in the squares made by the lattice. The crust was browned, and the smell was amazing. I pulled out an oven mitt from the nearby drawer and slipped it on. "Mom's asleep," I said as I pulled out the pie and set it onto the counter. I used my knee to close the oven and then turned to face Patty.

"She's sleeping?" she asked as she leaned her hip against the counter and folded her arms.

I nodded. My stomach dropped as the words I was going to have to say next formed in my mind. I hated saying the words. I wanted to pretend that this wasn't part of my life. But it was. And I couldn't hide from it even if I wanted to.

"My mom has cancer." The words came out barely a whisper.

Patty's eyebrows went up. "I'm so sorry," she said.

A response that I'd grown used to. I once replied, "Why? What did you do?" but learned very quickly that humor wasn't an expected response to that comment, so I just stuck to pinched lips and a soft nod.

"Yeah," I said quietly.

We stood there in silence for a few seconds before I blew out my breath. I was ready to move on with this conversation. "So, what did you bring?" I asked as I moved over to the plastic bag she brought and peered inside.

"Powdered doughnuts," she said. "But that was because I didn't know that you'd be making a pie." Her gaze was focused on the steaming, fruity, goodness that was cooling next to the oven.

"It's our family recipe. And it's amazing." I grabbed a few paper plates from the stack on the counter and moved to dish up the pie.

Patty and I talked and ate for the next hour. It was so nice, just relaxing in the kitchen, eating pie, and chatting. Patty and I had a lot in common and by the time we were completely stuffed on pie and standing to throw away our plates, the unspoken result of our conversation was we were best friends.

My time here in Glories Bluff was going to be a lot better with Patty in my life.

She said goodbye just as Mom walked groggily into the kitchen. They greeted each other, and when I mentioned to Mom that Patty loved Tarot cards, they fell into a loud and laughing conversation about the intricacies of that art form.

I smiled as I scooped up a pie piece for Mom, enjoying

the trill of their conversation. It was a moment I was trying to solidify in my memory. I wanted to never forget how I felt right now, in this kitchen.

Even though the realization of my future lingered forever in the back of my mind, tonight, I was going to force it into the darkness.

Tonight, I was going to live for the present.

7

SUSIE

I was left alone in the kitchen once Patty left to go home and Mom declared she was taking a bath and heading to bed. I gave them each a hug and then settled onto the kitchen chair with my phone, waiting for the motivation to get up and do the dishes.

I knew if I didn't get them done, Mom was going to feel the obligation to do it tomorrow, and it would zap most of her energy. Not wanting to add undue stress to my mother, I was determined to finish the dishes at some point tonight. Even though my eyes were drooping closed as I sat there.

My head fell forward with enough momentum for my eyes to pop open. "Time to get up," I said as I set my phone down on the table and stood. After picking a song on our family playlist, I flipped on the faucet in the kitchen and started working.

I was humming and rinsing when I heard the back door open and two male voices grow louder. I glanced over my shoulder to see Blake and Paul walk in. Paul looked tired, but Blake was smiling—as usual. When his gaze met mine, it widened.

"Good evening," he said with a deep, flourishing bow.

I nodded in his direction and then turned my focus to scraping off dried on bits of food from the pan we'd used this morning to make eggs. "Did you guys have a good night?" I asked.

Paul just shrugged and then excused himself. I hated how withdrawn he'd become. When it came to coping with Mom's illness, his response was to withdraw. Which was so strange to me. I wanted to do as much as I could with Mom while I had the time.

My gaze shifted to Blake who was standing in the middle of the kitchen with a goofy smile on his face. It was strange, him looking at me like he was. It made me blush.

"Are you heading out then?" I asked, hoping he'd give me the answer I wanted. I was tired, and honestly, I didn't want to spend the next however long trying to figure out what he meant by the words he *wasn't* saying. And I certainly didn't want to chat about our game plan when it came to Hannah.

I was ready to finish the dishes, climb into my pajamas, and shut the world out.

"Naw." His voice startled me. I turned to see him standing next to me with a dish towel in hand. "Are they ready?" he asked, picking up one of my freshly rinsed pans.

It took me a moment to realize what he was doing. When I did, I quickly nodded so that he didn't get suspicious of my sudden reaction. "Yeah."

"Wonderful."

We worked side by side, me washing and rinsing the dishes and then him coming from behind me to dry. My gaze kept wandering over to him until finally, I couldn't hold my questions in.

"This is how you wanted to spend your Monday night?" I waved my hand around the kitchen, shaking bubbles loose as I did. A clump landed on my nose, and I went to wipe it away, but a dish towel beat me to it.

I stood there, frozen, watching Blake reach up to dust them off my nose. His gaze became focused as he swiped the fabric back and forth. I couldn't breathe. I couldn't think. All I could do was stand there.

His gaze shifted from my nose to my gaze. He smiled at first, and then a moment later, his expression deepened as he studied me. And then, his hand dropped, and he took a step back.

"Sorry. Had the towel, thought I'd help out."

As he moved back, oxygen filled my body, and I could find the ability to breathe again. Not sure what to say, I just nodded and turned to focus back on the dishes in front of me.

Realizing that I was going to have to say something, I

cleared my throat. "It's okay. I'm okay. It's not a problem." I pinched my lips together. It was obvious that I wasn't going to be able to mentally stop my words, so I was going to have to physically do it.

With my mouth shut, no nonsensical and stupid words could come out.

Blake didn't respond right away which sent me into a tailspin. Had I said the wrong thing? Did he suddenly realize how much of a dork I was? I paused before I peeked over my shoulder at him.

He didn't seem mad or disappointed. Instead, he was just smiling. Not in a creeper way, but in a soft, affectionate way.

Not liking how vulnerable I felt right now, I turned back to the water. "What?" I finally asked. It felt like I was standing here, completely exposed to Blake. Why was he smiling like that? Why was he even here?

He liked Hannah, not me. Why wasn't he in her kitchen, staring at her? Doing her dishes?

He was so confusing to me, and it was exhausting me to try to figure him out.

His chuckle was soft and sounded right next to me. He grabbed a dish and started drying again. "Nothing."

Oh no. There was no way I was going to stand here, mentally sweating from his presence only for him to respond that way. I scoffed, hoping he'd pick up on my nonverbal cues.

"What?"

Good. It worked.

I glared over at him. "Nothing," I responded, hoping to give him a taste of his own medicine.

He was quiet for a moment before he shrugged and said, "Okay."

He set his dish towel down on the counter and picked up the stack of pans. Then he turned and glanced around at the cabinets behind us.

I was not satisfied with that answer. "What do you mean, okay?" I asked as I left my post at the sink and followed after him. He'd zoned in on the cabinet next to the oven and pulled it open. I wasn't even sure that was where we were even going to house the pans, but right now, I didn't care.

He paused before he glanced up at me in an annoyingly nonchalant way. "I mean it in the way the word is normally used. Okay. Fine. Sounds good." He shrugged. "Take your pick."

I stared at him, wanting to reach out and shake him. But I knew what touching him would do to me. With how tired I was, I knew I wasn't going to be able to control my reaction to that connection. So, I was going to keep my hands at my sides.

Realizing that there was no way that I was going to be able to express myself without sounding crazy, I just sighed and headed back to the sink. Blake was confusing, and I was ready to try my hardest to forget him.

I felt his presence when he approached. It was like a

warm shadow, and I hated that I noticed it. This relationship may be fake in theory, but it was becoming real to me, and I hated that.

My heart was breaking from Mom already. I didn't need my heart broken from a guy as well.

"We should make up some rules," I said as I shifted away from him and grabbed the mixing bowl to wash.

"Rules?"

I nodded. "We're in a fake relationship. We need to make rules." I paused and glanced out the window. "Like, you aren't going to pay for me."

He scoffed. "Yeah, not going to happen."

I glanced over at him. "What? Why?"

He'd picked up a wooden spoon and dried it. "My grandfather taught me to hold doors and pay for women's food." He paused before meeting my gaze. "And I'm more terrified of him haunting me from the grave than you and your adorable little scowl."

My cheeks heated. I knew he was teasing me, but for some reason, my body felt as if he were flirting. And I *hated* that I reacted this way.

I raised my finger and pointed at him. "See. This right here. This is what I'm talking about." I quickly dried my hands on my shirt and dug through the opened "junk drawer" box and found a pen and a scrap piece of paper. I wrote RULES at the top.

"Rule number one, no flirting." I paused. What was I

doing? Why had I said that word? What if he wasn't flirting? What if this was how he treated every girl?

He sucked in his breath. "Not sure I can do that, little Susie."

"Why?"

He shrugged. "Flirting is in my DNA."

Great. Here he was, admitting to me that he was a big flirt—which I already knew—but it was hard to actually hear it. There was a part of me—a very small part—that wanted to believe that he treated me differently.

Apparently not.

But this was good. This was going to help ground me in reality.

"Well, you're going to have to put it on hold for this," I said as I turned my pen over and tapped it on the counter in front of me.

Blake held my gaze. I could actually see the internal struggle going on inside of it. This was going to be really hard for him.

"No flirting?" he asked with a pained tone.

I nodded. "None. Zip. Zilch. Take your pick."

He raised his finger. "Hey, no flirting."

I dropped my jaw. "I wasn't flirting." *Was I?* Maybe I was. And he was right. If I was going to demand that he didn't flirt, I couldn't do it either.

I forced my expression to somber. "You're right. I will keep from flirting." I quirked an eyebrow. "Can you?"

He closed his eyes for a moment, took in a deep breath, and then nodded. "I can," he whispered.

"Good." I tapped the end of the pen on my chin as I thought of the next rule. "No...er..." How was I going to say this? How does one say there should be no physical contact? Was he going to think I was crazy?

I decided to face it head on. "No kissing." My cheeks heated at those two little words.

His silence surprised me. I glanced up to see him studying me. His expression was hard to read, and the look in his eyes even harder. Was he okay with this? Upset? Indifferent?

"Kissing?" He finally asked after what felt like an eternity.

I nodded. This was a rule I was determined to stick to. I was okay with faking a relationship to make Mom happy. I was even okay with faking a relationship to help Blake win back Hannah. But I wasn't okay with faking a relationship that ended in my heartbreak. And if I kissed Blake...

My gaze drifted down to his lips and held there for a moment. I'd never realized until now that he had perfect lips. They were full and soft. I wondered what they would feel like if I kissed them. The last boy I'd kissed was the summer before my sophomore year. It was rushed and sloppy, and I spent the rest of the night wiping his spit from my face.

But Blake. Blake looked like the kind of guy that knew

what to do.

"No kissing?" he asked again after he cleared his throat.

I ripped my gaze from his mouth and glanced back up, nodding quickly. "No kissing at all."

He pushed his hand through his hair and looked away. Then he shrugged. "If that's what you want."

I wanted to ask him if that was what he wanted as well but decided that it was time we moved on from the discussion of our lips meeting. So, I focus my attention on writing those two words down.

"Rule number three," I said as I wrote the number 3 on the paper. "Everyone buys their own things."

"Nope. Veto."

I sighed as I glanced over at him. "What? Why?"

He pointed toward the ceiling. "I told you. I will be haunted by my grandfather. You will let me pay when we go out."

I glowered at him and then sighed. "Well, I guess it's only fair. After all, you better get used to spending money. *Hannah* doesn't look like the kind of girl who likes Taco Bell and nights in."

I hadn't realized that my perfect idea of a date had slipped out until I saw Blake's intrigued expression. To keep that part of my personality a secret, I hurried to add, "Like girls I know."

"Girls you know?"

I shrugged. "Just because New York has fashion week,

doesn't mean that the girls there don't like the simple delicacies of life."

"Taco Bell is a delicacy?"

I really needed to stop talking. "Anyway, it's good for you to get used to spending money on Hannah." There, I'd successfully returned the conversation to Blake and his ex-girlfriend.

"Tell me what you *really* think of Hannah," he teased.

I eyed him. Did he really want to know? "You don't want to know what I think," I muttered as I drew a figure eight in the corner of the paper.

"I do."

I glanced up. Blake looked earnest as he studied me. Did he really care? I waited as I mulled over my words. This entire conversation had not gone the way I wanted it to, and I was fairly certain that was because I wasn't thinking before I spoke. And with a question like this, I wanted to choose my reaction carefully.

"I think you can do better." The words lingered in the air after I spoke them. I waited, holding my breath for his answer. Was that the wrong thing to say? I wasn't sure.

It was true if anything. From what I could see, she didn't deserve him. He was too good for her.

"You got that from the few times you saw her today?"

My throat went dry. It *had* been the wrong thing to say. I swallowed, hoping that my spit could help. It didn't. So, I stood and moved to grab a cup and fill it with water. "Call it girl intuition," I said as I set the cup down.

He didn't respond right away. It looked like he was chewing on my words. "So, what kind of girl do you think I could get?" He stepped closer, his expression turning earnest. Like he really wanted to know.

My cheeks heated as he closed the distance between us. I was certain it was because he felt vulnerable right now. After all, his cocky persona had faded and for the first time since we moved here, he looked earnest. Like this was a mystery that he wanted to solve for himself.

I wanted to speak. I did. But I couldn't find the words. All I could think was…me.

But that was stupid and ridiculous and something that should not be on my mind at all. He was my brother's friend, and he was still in love with his ex-girlfriend. The last thing he was even thinking about was me. I was the dorky girl that he knew growing up, and I was a means to the end of his single life.

I needed to keep those facts in the forefront of my mind. If not, I was going to spiral, and I knew at the end, I would be the one with a broken heart.

Not him.

"Mrs. Prutrella," I said before turning to focus back on the paper that I'd been writing our list on.

Blake was silent for a moment. "The librarian?"

My cheeks heated, and I could feel a smile start to emerge. But I remembered rule number one, so I did my best to stifle it. "She'd be perfect for you," I said as I doodled a drawing on the corner of the paper.

"Let me get this straight. Out of everyone at Glories Bluff High, a sixty-year-old woman who is missing a front tooth and looks like she could be Mrs. Claus is the person you could see me with."

I peeked over at him and almost broke out in laughter. His eyes were wide, and he looked like a crazed person as he stared me down. I took in a deep breath as I turned to face him.

"One hundred percent."

Blake held my gaze before he shook his head. "You're crazy, you know that?"

I shrugged. "Crazy or spot on."

He harrumphed next to me, folding his arms in front of him and glaring at me.

I tapped the list and smiled over at him. "This is good. I feel better. Do you?"

He continued his scowl. "Whatever you want."

"Good." I nodded and stood to head over to the sink to finish the dishes.

Even though I wanted to walk back my words about Mrs. Prutrella, I knew I couldn't. I was already opening up my heart despite my efforts to keep it closed. If I was this weak at the beginning of our fake relationship, what was I going to do every day that I spent with him?

No. To keep my heart intact, I needed to keep him as far away as I possibly could.

I needed to protect myself.

Period.

8

SUSIE

Blake did so good sticking to our rules at school the next day that I almost bought him a sucker as a reward. He controlled his flirty tendencies to a palpable amount. Patty was okay with being around him, yet Hannah was gradually becoming more and more jealous.

I could tell by the death glares she shot my way.

I was lingering by my locker at the end of the day when Blake suddenly appeared next to me. He had a wide smile on his lips as he leaned against the locker next to mine and studied me.

I'd been lost in the book that I was reading, and when I glanced over at him and met his gaze, my cheeks heated. I quickly closed my book and set it inside my backpack. "What's up?"

He furrowed his brow. "How do you feel about horses?"

I shrugged. "I like them."

"Wanna come to my house and go for a ride?"

I furrowed my brow. "Why?"

He scoffed. "Do I need a reason?"

I glanced over at him, giving him an *"Are you serious?"* look. "Kind of."

He turned to rest his back against the lockers and folded his arms. "I hear that Hannah and others are heading to Devil's Pond." His voice was quiet as if he were ashamed of what he was saying.

And I'll admit, his words did cut me, but I quickly moved on from that. "Let's do it," I said as I shouldered my backpack and slammed my locker shut. "It'll be fun." I forced a smile.

Blake's eyebrows went up. "It will?"

I nodded. "Yep."

He pushed off the locker he was leaning against and clapped his hands. "Perfect. I'll pick you up in an hour?"

"From my house?"

He nodded.

I shrugged. "Or I can drive to your house. Probably would be easier since you won't need to drive to my house just to go back to yours."

I could see the internal struggle inside of him. The words "haunted by my grandfather" floated around inside my mind. But I was going to hold steady. I needed some autonomy from Blake. I knew he wanted to appease his old fashioned relative, but I needed a way out in case things got too intense.

He finally sighed and nodded. "Works for me. See you there at four?"

"Perfect."

He lingered for a few moments before he nodded and headed down the hallway. With him gone, I pulled out my phone to see that Paul had texted that he was ready to leave and for me to meet him at the car.

When I got there, Paul was already inside with the radio blaring. I slipped onto the passenger seat, and he peeled out of the parking lot. I wanted to ask him what was bothering him. He was becoming more and more aloof. I thought it was about the move and Mom, but now I was starting to think it was something different.

He didn't talk to me the entire drive home. When he parked in the driveway, he pulled the keys from the engine and moved to get out.

"Actually," I hurried to say. Once Paul was locked in his room, he wasn't ever going to come out.

He paused and glanced over his shoulder with an annoyed and expectant look. "What?"

"Can I get the keys? I...have somewhere to be in an hour."

He glanced down, and I could see the internal struggle going on inside of him. He wanted out of the car, but he didn't want to give me the keys. Finally, he tossed them into my lap and was out of the car and slamming the door before I could respond.

I blew out my breath as I collapsed against the seat. I was going to have to do some digging when it came to my big brother. Something was wrong, and I just wasn't sure what.

With the keys in hand, I climbed out of the car. Mom was in the kitchen with a few water glasses laid out in front of her. Her crystals were out, and she was polishing them before dropping them into the water.

"How'd school go, sweetie?" she asked. She was wearing a multicolored scarf today and a big flowy dress. She looked exactly like the type of person you would think would believe in moon crystals and rejuvenating water.

I loved my mom. So much so that I didn't want to leave. I had half a mind to take out my phone and text Blake that I needed to cancel. After all, how many moments like this did I have left? Was I ready to walk out on my mom to be with a boy who wanted to get back his ex?

"Oh no, what's wrong?"

I set the keys down on the counter and my backpack down on the ground in front of them. "Nothing. Just changing my plans."

"You had plans?" I shot her an exasperated look, to which she just grinned. "I'm joking." Then she studied me. "What plans are you changing?"

My head was already in the fridge as I dug around for some yogurt. Mom must have had an energy spike today because the kitchen looked more put together and we had new food in the fridge. "Did you go to the store?" I asked when I located a dark chocolate cherry yogurt and shut the fridge behind me.

"I ordered online, and don't change the subject Susan."

From the corner of my eye, I saw Mom raise her finger and point it at me.

I popped the top of the yogurt, dug around until I found a clean spoon, and then took a big bite. I widened my eyes as I studied her. I couldn't talk if I was eating.

Mom didn't look like she minded. She was busy with her crystals, and she really had no place to go. If it came down to who could wait the longest, that would be her.

Drat.

I finished off my yogurt and dumped the carton into the trash. After I rinsed off the spoon and slipped it into the dishwasher, I turned to face her. "Blake wants me to ride horses with him tonight."

Mom's eyes widened. "Really? That sounds fun. Why don't you want to go?"

I gave her an *"Are you serious?"* look. "Because I want to be here with you."

Mom paused. Her gaze remained on the crystals in front of her. I could tell that she didn't like that answer and was choosing her words carefully. Even if I wanted to fight her, I knew that she was going to win.

"You should go. You made a commitment to help him with Hannah." She raised her gaze to meet mine.

I wanted to tell her that she was crazy. That I didn't want to go with Blake because I was rapidly finding myself feeling things for him that I didn't want to feel. Plus, I wanted to stay here with her.

"But—"

"Susie, I want to see you happy and a normal teenager. I can't have you here waiting for me to..." Her voice trailed off, but the word she was about to say lingered in the air.

I knew it, and so did she.

Die.

She didn't want me to wait around for her to *die*. Ugh. I hated that word. I hated that it even needed to be said in a sentence. I needed my mom more than anything, yet it felt as if we were just living on borrowed time.

And nothing I did stopped anything.

"But mom..." My voice cracked as tears started to form in my eyes. I blinked a few times, hoping to dispel them.

Mom shook her head. "You need to go. I need you to go, and Blake needs you to go." She smiled at me, but I could still see the sadness in her eyes. "It'll be good for you, and I'll be here, thinking of all the fun you'll be having." She pressed her lips together.

I crossed the room and wrapped my arms around her.

"Are you sure?" All she needed to say was no, and I would cancel right now. If she wanted me around, I was happy to stay home.

Mom pulled back and rested her hands on my cheeks. She smiled at me, and through her sorrow and exhaustion, I could see her hope. She loved me and wanted good things for me. Even though I doubted she understood how much I needed to stay by her, I was willing to leave if that was what she wanted.

"Go. I'll be fine."

I nodded, a single tear slipping down my cheek. Not wanting it to turn into a full-blown tear fest, I pulled back, cleared my throat, and focused my attention on Mom's moon crystals. "Need any help? I don't need to leave for an hour."

Mom turned her attention back to what she was doing as well. "That would be wonderful."

The hour passed too quickly, and I contemplated telling Mom that I was happy to stay but then pushed that thought out. Instead, I slipped off the barstool, gave her a kiss, and headed into my room to find my swimsuit that was tucked away in one of my boxes.

It took a few minutes, but once I located it, I slipped into it and then wore a tank and shorts over it. I grabbed my keys, said goodbye to Mom, and headed out the door.

I had to use my navigation to find Blake's house. He lived on the outskirts of town. His house was a small farmhouse with chickens that dotted the land. I smiled as I turned off the engine and climbed out.

A deep bark startled me, and I turned, half contemplating climbing back into my car and heading home. A large, white, fluffy dog with wise eyes glared up at me.

"Ah, give her a break, Marshmallow," Blake's voice sounded from the house.

I glanced up to see him coming down the deck stairs. He had on swim trunks and a white t-shirt which made his tan stand out more than ever. It took me a minute to gather my thoughts and rip my gaze away from him. Thankfully, he seemed more focused on getting Marshmallow to leave me alone than to notice.

"You found the place," he said as he extended out his hands.

Marshmallow seemed to realize that I was no longer a threat and moved to lay in the shade of a nearby tree.

"Yeah. It wasn't too hard."

Blake was studying me through his squinted eyes. The sun was directly behind me, which I appreciated. It made me feel less vulnerable to him when I could only see half his gaze.

"Everything okay?" he asked as he moved to rest his hand on the hood of my car. That brought his body and chest closer to me.

I swallowed, wanting to step back but fearing what that would reveal to him. "Yeah. It's hard leaving Mom, but she told me I had to come."

Blake's expression faltered, which confused me. It almost seemed that he was disappointed that I needed Mom to tell me to come. Which was strange. After all, Mom was the one who pitched the idea of us fake dating to begin with.

I brushed his reaction to the side and focused on what I was here for. We were going to ride out to some lake and make Hannah jealous. He couldn't get upset with me if I was here to do the one thing we'd agreed upon. And I didn't need to feel bad if I wasn't jumping up and down to do said thing.

Thankfully, Blake moved on. He clapped his hands together and then rubbed them like he was a maniacal character in a murder mystery. His grin made me laugh as I studied him.

"Are you going to murder me?" I asked as I took a step back.

He shook his head and reached out to grab my hand. "Come on. Let's go introduce you to Honey."

I felt confused until he dragged me to the nearby barn, and then I realized that Honey was a horse. The barn was surprisingly tidy when he led me inside. There were four stalls, two on each side. One was empty, the other three had horses inside. They were eating and looking at me suspiciously.

I wasn't a normally anxious person but standing next to a horse that was as tall as I was, made me nervous. Especially when they were giving me the stink eye. I was certain, one swift kick, and I would be smashed against the wall.

"You okay?" Blake asked. He'd returned with a saddle in hand.

I nodded, swallowing hard to dispel my nerves. "Yeah, I think so." Then I leaned into him so the horse couldn't hear me. "Do they normally look like this?"

His gaze drifted over to Honey. "Look like what?" he asked. His tone matched mine, and when he leaned in, shivers cascaded across my skin.

Dang it.

Why did this keep happening? I swear, I was a glutton for punishment.

Forcing myself to push out the thoughts of attraction that seemed to plague my mind, I straightened and focused. "She looks like I owe her money."

Blake laughed, startling the horse and me. I glowered at him. If the horse didn't like me before, Blake's sudden outburst wasn't going to win me points. I shushed him, but he didn't pay me any mind. Instead, he heaved the saddle onto Honey's back and began to strap it on.

I kept my distance, watching Honey's every move. But she seemed unaffected by what was going on and continued eating. Her demeanor helped calm me, and I found my muscles relaxing.

"Blake?"

A deep, male voice called into the barn. And just like that, Blake's shoulders tightened, and a strained look crossed over his face. His gaze flicked from me to the front of the barn where the voice came from.

"Yeah, Dad?"

Dad. Blake's dad. I moved to see, but suddenly, Blake's hands were on my shoulders, and he was pushing me into the far corner of Honey's stall. His hands pressed on either side of my head, and the pleading look in his gaze made my heart pound. He brought his finger up to his lips and gave me the universal *shush* signal.

"What are you doing?" his dad asked.

Blake closed his eyes but kept me pressed against the wall. "I'm taking Honey out for a ride." He winced as if he realized he'd just made a fatal mistake.

"Honey?"

"Yeah."

Silence.

Blake opened his eyes, and I had not been prepared for that. They were a stormy blue, a stark contrast from his flirty sky blue color that I'd gotten used to. There was something going on here. Something he wasn't telling me. And something he was hiding from the rest of the world.

Our conversations about him not wanting to go home or not being missed came rushing back to me. Did they have something to do with his dad?

He must have sensed my questions, because he furrowed his eyebrows as he deepened his gaze. There was a depth there that took my breath away.

"Fine. Just have her back before dark," his dad said, breaking the trance we seemed to be under.

Blake turned in the direction of his dad's voice and said, "Okay."

I held my breath, waiting for another response, but nothing came. I glanced back at Blake who was staring at me, but as soon as our gazes met, he pushed away from the wall, mumbling, "Sorry," as he did.

He disappeared around the corner of the stall, and I stood there feeling completely discombobulated. I was cold from the lack of warmth his body had given me. I felt lightheaded from how close he'd been to me.

My heart was pounding from the intensity of his stare.

What had that been?

"He's gone," Blake said as he reappeared.

Not wanting him to know what his presence had done to me, I forced a relaxed expression and nodded. "Oh, okay."

Blake kept his focus on the horse, but I could tell that he wanted to say more. He was agitated, and I hated that. I wished he would just talk to me. We were friends. I could keep his secret.

He patted Honey's shoulder and then glanced over at me. "We're going to have to ride together," he said as he extended his hand.

"Sure," I said as I slipped my hand into his. I wanted to avoid touching him at all costs, but I didn't trust my ability to climb onto the horse without falling over the other side. I would brave the ripples of feeling that were coursing through my hand from his touch.

I swung my leg over the saddle and situated myself there.

Then, before I could process what was happening, Blake had swung himself up onto Honey behind me, his arm wrapping around my waist.

My whole body stiffened. "What are you doing?" I asked.

I could feel Blake's head shift as if he were looking at me. His soft chuckle tickled my ear. "We have to ride together," he said. His voice was soft, and his breath was warm on my skin.

Oh. That's what he meant when he said ride together. I just figured he meant I was going to have to stay with him while he rode his own horse.

Blake hesitated as he held Honey's reins in his hands. "Is that okay?"

We were so close that I could feel his voice as it reverberated in his chest. His body warmth penetrated my whole back as he pressed his chest against me. His arm was tight around my stomach, and I feared he could feel my own heartbeat. That he would know exactly how I felt about him.

How I was trying desperately not to feel about him.

But we were here, and his body next to mine felt incredible. I felt warm and protected, and call me crazy, but I didn't want to give that up.

Not right now.

For the next hour, I was going to enjoy this.

I was going to enjoy myself.

And then I would manage my feelings for Blake.

Then I would face reality.

9

SUSIE

Blake quickly led Honey out of the barn and across the field that surrounded his house. I could tell that he was nervous about being spotted, so I let him do what he needed to in order to get us safely into the tree line on the far end of his property.

Once we were protected, he slowed Honey to a trot, and I could feel his muscles relax. He still kept a tight hold of me, but his demeanor changed.

Which helped me relax. I was enjoying this ride—even if I hadn't expected we would ride horses this way. I liked being this close to Blake, and I was beginning to realize that the more time I spent with Blake, the harder it was going to be for me to walk away once he and Hannah were together.

That thought made me want to pull away.

I was already trying to get used to being without Mom. Why was I introducing more heartbreak into my life?

Panic set it. I wasn't helping myself by falling for Blake. Besides, he didn't see me this way. He wanted Hannah, and I was just a means to that end. I was a fool to let myself indulge in thoughts of anything but friendship with Blake.

"So, where are we meeting Hannah?" I asked. I hated that my voice sounded weak. Like I was worried or even cared about what he was about to say. But bringing her up helped me remember what I was doing.

It helped me remember the point to all of this time we were spending together.

Blake was quiet for a moment, and I could tell from the corner of my eye, that he'd turned his attention to me. He cleared his throat, and I could feel the rumble in his chest once more.

The desire to get off this horse and to give myself some space from him grew inside of my gut. But I was fairly certain he would notice if I suddenly bailed.

I was stuck, so the best thing I could do was remind myself of Hannah. She needed to stay in the forefront of my mind.

"At the lake, just on the other side of these trees," he said.

"And how much longer?"

He was quiet. "Are you okay?"

No. I wasn't okay. I wasn't okay with anything in my

life right now. I wanted to hide from the reality that I'd found myself in. I wanted Mom to get better. I wanted to know that she would be there for me on graduation day. Or my wedding day. Or the birth of my first child.

I wanted to feel settled and like I belonged. I wanted Blake to like me and not Hannah. I wanted my brother to figure his crap out, so he could be a support to me and not a hinderance.

I wanted my life to be simple and not the mess that it'd become.

But I couldn't say those things to Blake, even though I wanted to. We weren't boyfriend and girlfriend. I wasn't even sure if we were friends. After all, I'd been thrown into this life in Montana so fast, that I hadn't even had time to breathe.

"I'm getting nauseous," I whispered. I wanted Blake to believe it was because of the movement from the horse, but it wasn't only that. I needed space from him. From the crapshoot that was my life.

"What can I do to help?" he asked.

"Maybe get down?"

He clicked his tongue and pulled back on Honey's reins. Before I could blink, he was slipping off, and his feet landed on the ground. I wasn't sure where to look, so I kept my gaze forward. Blake didn't say anything as he walked next to the horse.

I felt stupid, making him walk like this. But I was in

self-preservation mode. I needed the distance to get my head on straight.

"Feel better?" he asked after a few minutes of silence.

I nodded. "Yeah. Thanks."

He glanced up at me, his smile taking my breath away. Ugh. Why was I such a mess? Falling for my fake boyfriend was ridiculous. I had a one-way ticket to heartbreak. The worst part of it all? Blake was nice, yet had no idea how much turmoil he was putting me through.

All because I was too weak to keep my heart contained.

"I never said thank you for helping me."

I was confused. "With what?"

He shrugged as he reached out and grabbed some leaves off a nearby branch. "For agreeing to help me with Hannah. I'm sure this wasn't what you wanted, but I'm glad you agreed."

I wanted to tell him that it originally started because I wanted Mom to be happy, but I kept that to myself. Regardless of how I felt about him, I did want to see him settled. And if that meant helping him win back his ex, then I would help him win her back.

I leaned my arm forward and rested it on the saddle. "Do you think it's working?" I felt dumb asking a question that I already knew the answer to. Hannah had an uncanny ability to make me feel tiny every time I was around her. If that didn't speak to her feelings for Blake, I didn't know what did.

He shrugged. "I think so. But Hannah's always been like this. She wants what she can't have." He glanced up at me. "And right now, I'm the one thing she can't have."

There was a depth to his voice, a deepness in his gaze, that had me sitting upright. My breath caught in my throat as his words played over and over in my mind. She can't have him? Why?

"Because we're fake dating?" I asked. I needed to know the reason he said that.

He paused, his gaze holding mine for a moment before he nodded. "Of course."

I felt both relieved and crushed at the same time. I wanted him to say there was a different reason, but I also wanted things to be simple. Keeping our focus on the reason we originally started this relationship seemed like our best option.

"Well, from what I can see, Hannah is extremely interested. And I think if we keep at it for a few days more, she'll be knocking on your door."

"You're okay with that?" He peeked up at me.

No, but I was going to have to be. "Pssh. I'm doing great. It's been fun watching her squirm."

He squinted up at me. "Oh, you're brutal."

I shrugged. "When I have to be."

The trees broke apart, revealing a large, gleaming lake. The water was calm and blue, and the sun glistened off its surface making it look as if it were made of diamonds.

"Wow," I whispered as Blake clicked his tongue once more, and Honey stopped moving.

"It's amazing, isn't it?" Blake was by my side, holding his hand up for me to take.

I slipped to the ground but didn't break my gaze away from the scene that spread out in front of me. "I should bring Mom here," I whispered.

Blake led Honey over to a fallen tree and tied her to it. She didn't waste any time, dipping her head down to drink. Once she was taken care of, Blake began pulling his shirt off.

My cheeks heated as I turned my attention away from him and focused back on the lake that was now rippling from Honey's drinking.

"Where's Hannah?" I asked.

Blake's splashing caused me to turn. He was running into the lake, and as soon as he was deep enough, he dipped down until only his head was showing. "Who knows? We can go looking for her once we've cooled down." Then he shrugged, his shoulders appearing and then disappearing under the surface of the water. "Besides, aren't we supposed to be here just the two of us?" His wink caused my skin to warm once more.

I needed to get into the water before my body gave away how I felt about him. Not sure if he was watching or not, I pushed all of my shy thoughts from my mind and slipped off my tank and shorts. Then I half ran, half walked into the water. When I could, I dipped down and let the cool temperature rush over me.

Blake was smiling at me when I finally reached him. His hair was wet, and droplets of water glistened on his skin. His dark lashes were wet and accentuated his blue eyes.

I narrowed my eyes, not sure why he was grinning like he was. "What?" I asked as I swished my hands around underneath the water's surface.

He chuckled. "Nothing." He paused. "Actually, I was just thinking how much things have changed since we were kids and living in New York."

I thought back to the few memories I had of his family living by us. I didn't have a lot, but the ones I did have involved him and Paul, running as fast as they could away from me. Things really had changed.

"Yeah. I'm no longer the girl with cooties, am I?" I asked as I lifted my hand to the surface and splashed him.

Blake was taken off guard, his mouth opening as he stared at me. "I never said you had cooties."

I squinted my left eye and pursed my lips. "I think you did."

"I would have never said that about a person."

I chuckled, splashing him again. "You and Paul used to run away from me, screaming about how I was going to get you two sick." I stepped closer to him, this time, aiming the water so it went directly in his face.

Blake sputtered and then returned fire. "I would have never said that about you."

"Well, you did," I said after wiping my face and then splashing him again.

"If I'd known that you would be doing this, I wouldn't have said that things have changed." Suddenly, his fingers wrapped around my wrist, and I was being pulled toward him.

I pressed my hands against his chest to brace myself, but that had been a mistake. The warmth of his skin mixed with the beating of his heart. It was a sensation that I'd never experienced before, and I didn't want it to end.

We stood there, frozen in the water. His arm was wrapped around my waist as his other hand held tight to my wrist. It was as if he had been just as startled by the tension that seemed to magnify one hundred-fold.

"Blake," I whispered, desperate to clear the tense air between us. I was moments away from slipping down the cliff of my feelings for him. One more step, and I was gone.

His gaze met mine, and I realized just how close we were together. Our lips were mere inches away from each other. All I would need to do was rise up onto my tip toes and...

Get a grip.

Kissing me was the last thing on his mind.

"Blake," I tried again, this time, more forceful.

He blinked, and as if he'd been burned, he dropped both his hands and took a step back. "Yeah?"

The cool lake temperature surrounded me, making me shiver. I wrapped my arms around my chest and stood there, wishing that I could forget the way it felt when he held me. Wishing it could be like it had been when we were kids. Back before I ever had feelings for him.

"Sorry," he mumbled as he pushed his hand through his hair. "I got a little carried away."

I shook my head. "No, it's okay. It was my fault." I took in a deep breath. "I broke rule number one," I said.

He paused and then looked over at me. "Right. The rules."

I gave him a small smile as I wrapped my arms around my chest and dipped down blow the lake's surface. "It's best we keep to them."

He didn't respond verbally, but I saw him nod. Silence fell around us, and I glanced around, waiting and wishing Hannah would show up already.

"What time do you think she'll get here?" I squinted back at Blake.

He glanced around the water's edge at my question. "I'm not sure. She said she was coming here with her girlfriends, but..." He paused, raising his hand up to shield his eyes. "I don't see her."

Great. Not only was I completely confused by my feelings for Blake, but I was now stuck with him for an undetermined amount of time. Not only stuck with him, but I was stuck with him while we were both half-dressed and wet.

This was a recipe for disaster.

Blake pushed his hand through his hair. I was beginning to learn that he did this when he was nervous.

It was adorable.

I blinked a few times, forcing that word out of my mind. Blake was not adorable. Nothing Blake did was adorable. He wasn't allowed to be anything but Paul's friend and Hannah's soon-to-be boyfriend. If I allowed that word to confuse me, I was going to end up hurt.

And I didn't want to hurt.

"So, what's the plan?" I was on the edge of going insane. I needed to change topics, or I was going to slip into a slow state of madness.

Blake glanced over at me and then shrugged. "I hadn't really thought this through."

I sighed. Feelings of frustration grew inside me. Not toward Blake, but toward myself. I knew I shouldn't have come, yet I did anyway. Apparently, I'm a glutton for punishment.

"Wanna play twenty questions?" An age-old game that I remembered playing in the car as a kid. We would take Blake with us on road trips, and they always morphed into intense games of license plate bingo and twenty questions.

Blake narrowed his eyes. "Do you think you can win against the master?" He raised his arms above the water's surface and flexed.

My cheeks heated at the sight of his muscles. I dipped

down so that my mouth was below the lake's surface, hoping the coolness of the water would help soothe my cheeks. I nodded while willing him not to notice my reaction.

"You go first."

We played twenty questions for what felt like forever. We were on round five when I finally rose out of the water and started making my way to shore.

"Giving up?" Blake asked. His voice grew louder, and from the sound of splashing water, I knew he'd moved to follow me out.

I glanced over my shoulder. The sun was starting to set behind the trees, but its rays weren't shy. They broke through the leaves and caught the beads of water on his chest. He looked like he was glowing, and the light emphasized his chest.

Great.

"I was turning into a prune," I said as I moved to sit on a large rock. Honey glanced over at me with a bored expression. She'd found a patch of grass and was happily eating away. I reached out and gently petted her nose.

Blake chuckled as he moved to sit on the rock next to me. Thankfully, the sun had warmed its surface, heating me up. I knew it wasn't going to last forever, and with the setting sun, I had goosebumps running across my skin.

"Do you think she's coming?" I asked as I raised my hand to my arms and rubbed. When I turned to look at Blake, I caught him staring. Not in a creepy way, but in a way that made the butterflies in my stomach take flight and caused my entire body to warm.

He blinked and then dropped his gaze to the lake. "I'm not sure. I'm starting to think that she may have changed her mind."

I nodded. Just my luck.

"Are you not having a good time?" His voice was soft, and from the corner of my eye, I could see that his gaze had returned to me. "Even though this is all fake, I still want you to have a good time."

The earnestness in his voice made me smile. Not wanting to give my feelings away, I reached out and started to draw circles on the rock with my wet finger. The rock darkened where I ran my finger and then quickly faded from the heat.

"I'm having a good time," I whispered. There was so much to unpack in that statement. So much fear wrapped up in it. I wanted to run headfirst into the happiness that I felt when I was around Blake. But the guilt of being happy when Mom was sick, mixed with reality that none of this was real kept me sane.

But when he asked me questions like that. When he made me face my true feelings, I wanted to throw away all of my fear and just leap.

Leap into the happiness that was Blake.

Leap into a reality that I could never have.

The wind picked up, causing me to shiver. I glanced back over at him, willing myself to say the words I knew I needed to speak. I needed distance between us. It was the only way I was ever going to find happiness once Blake and Hannah were back together.

"I'm cold," I admitted, emphasizing my words by rubbing my arm closest to him.

His gaze dipped down, and a worry line emerged between his brows. "I'm so sorry," he said, instantly rising to his feet. "I packed no towels or anything." He glanced around. "Let's get back to my house."

He didn't give me a moment to speak. Instead, he was untying Honey and helping me up onto the saddle before I could say anything.

He handed me his shirt and demanded I put it on. I wanted to fight—there was no way wearing his shirt and smelling his cologne was going to help my current status—but he wouldn't take no for an answer, so I slipped it on.

10

SUSIE

The ride back to Blake's house was like sitting in a hot oven with all of my clothes on.

It wasn't that I wasn't still wet and cold from the lake—I was. But having Blake pressed against me as we rode Honey through the woods made me warmer than I wanted to admit.

Add to that the smell of his t-shirt and the softness of it against my skin—my nerves were a wreck. I wanted to melt into his body and jump down and run screaming from him at the same time.

I'd never felt so conflicted or in utter turmoil like I felt right now. What had started out as a favor to my mother had turned into something more. Something greater.

Blake pulled back on Honey's reins as she trotted into the barn. The two other horses were gone, and I wondered where they went. Memories of being pressed against the wall while Blake talked to his dad ran through my mind which only added to the confusion I felt about our relationship.

The confusion I felt about Blake.

"Let's get you warm," Blake said as he slid down onto the ground and then turned to face me.

I didn't want him to meet my gaze. I feared what he would discover if I let him in. So, I focused on standing, so I could swing my leg to the other side. I just needed to survive the next few minutes, and then I could make an excuse as to why I needed to leave and drive away from him and never look back.

Just as I moved to jump down, my foot caught, and suddenly, the ground was coming faster than I could stop it. I braced myself for impact, but it never happened. Instead, two arms wrapped around me, and I was pulled to Blake's chest.

It took me a moment to realize that I was now staring into Blake's eyes. My body pressed against his. His lips were centimeters from mine. I was suspended in the air, and the only thing holding me to the ground was Blake.

"Are you okay?" he asked. His voice had deepened and sent shivers down my spine.

I felt as if the entire world around us was slowing and all that existed was Blake and me. Everything else just faded into the background.

"Uh huh," I whispered. My gaze slipping down to

RULE #7 YOU CAN'T FAKE DATE YOUR BROTHER'S BE... 119

stare at his lips. His perfectly formed, soft looking lips. What would it feel like to kiss them?

Just as quickly as he'd caught me, suddenly, I was being set onto the ground. Blake took a step away from me, pushing his hands through his hair as he dropped his gaze. "Uh, good. I'm happy you're okay."

I couldn't help but stare at him. Was he feeling things too? What was happening? There was such a connection between us. An electrical current that I couldn't ignore. He had to feel it too.

Right?

Blake's gaze slowly rose up until he was staring at me. An unspoken desire flowed through that one single look. I knew I should break that connection. I knew that this was a big mistake, but I couldn't.

I wanted Blake.

I wanted this to be real.

"Let's get you some dry clothes," he said as he turned and headed through the barn.

I didn't have time to respond. He was gone before I could even part my lips to get any words out. All I could do was turn and follow after him.

His house was dark when I stepped into the kitchen. The only light was from the TV that was on in the living room. I moved to turn on the switch, but Blake caught my hand before I could do it. My gaze whipped to his as he stood there, his giant, warm hand wrapped around mine.

He was staring at our hands and didn't make a move to

drop mine. "Don't," he whispered as he slowly moved his gaze to meet mine.

My lips were parted, but I'd forgotten how to speak. So, I just nodded. He glanced back down at our hands and then slowly, loosened his grip. It was as if he were taking his time to release his hold on me.

I wanted him to stay. I wanted to hold his hand. I wanted to lean in and to see if he was feeling what I was feeling, but he was gone before I gathered the courage.

I stayed in the corner, fearing what I might do as Blake moved around the kitchen. He grabbed a few water bottles from the fridge and some snacks from the pantry. With all of his goodies gathered up in his arms, he nodded for me to follow him up the stairs.

Thankful for something to do other than stare at him as he moved in the darkness, I followed after him. All of the rooms in the small hallway that I found myself in were closed. Blake led me to the door at the farthest end of the hall and nodded toward it.

Realizing that there was no way he could open the door with everything he was holding, I moved to turn the handle. He pushed inside, and I lingered in the doorway. Did he really want me to go into his room?

Did I want to do that?

But then I felt like an idiot and followed after him.

Once inside, Blake dropped the food and water onto the bed and then moved to the small dresser in the corner and opened a drawer. I lingered by the door, so if I needed to, I could make a hasty retreat. Not because I feared what Blake might do to me, but I feared how hard I might fall for him if I allowed myself to get close.

Blake turned and scanned the room until he found me. Then he stepped up to me with a stack of clothes in his hands. "Here," he said.

It was dim in his room, but I swear I saw his cheeks turn pink. It was adorable.

"What do you want me to do with this?" I asked, my gaze never leaving his face. I needed him to guide me right now. It was as if I were frozen and my brain was stuck on repeat. The image that was flashing in my mind was Blake. His lips. His eyes.

I doubted I would even be able to relay my name correctly if he asked.

"Change into something warm." His voice was soft, and I could see his smile playing on his lips. He nodded toward the left side of the room.

"Right. Change," I whispered as I turned to see a half open door along the far wall.

Once inside, I shut the door and got started. I winced when I caught sight of my reflection. My hair was tousled, and my mascara had left dark splotches under my eyes. I groaned and hurried over to the sink where I turned on the water and began scrubbing.

Why had I agreed to do this? Why had I worn makeup? And why, *why* did I want Blake to kiss me as badly as I did? I wished I could just go back to when life was simple. All I wanted was to spend time with Mom and focus on adjusting to my new life.

Blake messed everything up. He confused me. He made me long to be touched. And he invaded my thoughts in a way that I wasn't okay with.

Because when I was thinking about him, I wasn't focused on Mom. I wasn't there with her. Tears of frustration clung to my eyes, and I used the warm water and soap on my cheeks to wash them away.

She wanted me to come. That's why I was here. I needed to remember that.

Once my face was dried and I'd raked my fingers through my damp hair, I slipped out of my swimsuit and into Blake's clothes. His shorts were too big on me, so I had to fold the waistband down a few times. As I stared at my reflection in the mirror, I realized that there was no way I could wear his t-shirt with no support underneath.

So, I grabbed my swimsuit and glanced around the bathroom. After looking under the sink, I managed to find a hair dryer—which I made note of to ask him why on earth he had one in his bathroom—and proceeded to dry my suit.

It took about five minutes, but I was able to get it dry enough to slip back on. Then I pulled on the black t-shirt and grey basketball shorts on over it. At least I now looked alive and that was all I could ask for.

It probably played in my favor. If I looked like a troll

who lived under the bridge, then he wouldn't stare at me like he'd done so many times today.

His expression was about to drive me crazy, so anything I could do to tamp that down, I was going to welcome.

I pulled open his bathroom door and found him sitting on his bed. He had changed into a pair of sweatpants and t-shirt and was softly strumming on his guitar. He paused and glanced over his shoulder, his expression softening when he saw me.

Butterflies were flying at the speed of light throughout my stomach as I studied him. I wasn't imagining this. He was looking at me like I was someone special to him.

Like…I mattered.

"They're a little big," I whispered as I pulled at the sides of his basketball shorts.

He didn't say anything. Instead, he slipped his guitar strap off his shoulders and moved to lean it against his bed. He stood and turned to focus on me.

"It looks great," he whispered and then, as if he realized what he'd just said, he winced and shoved his hands into his front pockets. "I mean, you look warm. That's good."

I wrapped one arm around my stomach and held my other arm with my hand. I gave him a shy smile, not sure where we were supposed to go from here. "I should probably head home—"

"Wanna watch a movie?"

We spoke over each other so quickly, that neither one of us knew what to do. We stood there with our lips pinched, looking at the other person.

"I've got some good classics," he finally said when it became apparent that I wasn't going to talk. He waved his hand toward the TV sitting on the dresser next to us.

I glanced over and then back to him, giving him a weak smile. There was no way that I was going to be able to mentally handle staying with him that long. If I was going to be able to walk away from this relationship with my heart intact, I needed to leave right now.

"I think I should get back to Mom. I know she doesn't like going to bed before I get home." That was sort of a lie. Lately, Mom had been falling asleep on the couch. In the past, she cared. Now, it wasn't that she wasn't bothered if I was out, but she really didn't have the energy to wait up.

"Oh. Yeah. Okay."

I hated how disappointed Blake sounded. I stepped forward, wanting to offer him some sort of solace, but I wasn't sure what I was actually going to do once I got close enough to him. I lingered back, waiting to see what he would do, but he didn't respond. Instead, he just shrugged and moved to pick up one of the water bottles on his bed.

"You can take this for the road," he said as he handed it in my direction.

Not wanting this evening to end, yet fighting the urge to sprint from his room, I took the water bottle from him and held it between my hands. The cold temperature shocked my system, jolting me from the lull my emotions had forced me into.

I needed a clearer head if I was going to continue being around Blake.

"Thanks." I gathered my things and moved to his door.

He looked as if he wanted to stop me but didn't know how. And I was fairly certain I didn't want him to. If he asked me to stay...I might.

I needed to get home to Mom.

"Thanks for a fun evening," I said, my fingers lingering on the door handle. Why wasn't I leaving? Why was I hanging out here? There was very little space separating me from the door. All I needed to do was turn the handle.

Yet I couldn't find the strength to do so.

He smiled and took a step toward me. There was something about the way he looked at me. Something about the way the left side of his lips tipped up higher than the right. There was something that he was thinking, but he wasn't going to act on.

Was it something I wanted him to act on?

"I'm going to go," I said, mustering my strength and pressing down on the handle. I needed to get out of here and fast. Walking down the hallway, out the front door, and over to my car was a blur. My heart was pounding so hard, I feared that my feet were going to turn around and force me back to his room.

Back to his arms.

I managed to climb into my car and close the door. I

started the engine and pulled out of his drive. The entire ride home, my body felt light. I wanted what I was feeling to be real. To mean something.

I feared I was the only one who felt this way. After all, he wanted Hannah back. And I wasn't Hannah. I was just his best friend's little sister. I was a nobody.

I sat in the driveway of my house for a few minutes while I composed myself. I'm sure Mom was going to have a lot of questions…if she was up.

I glanced through the windshield to her window. It was dark which made my hopes plummet. I wanted her to be awake. I wanted things to be normal. I wanted to be able to go into my house, find my healthy mom, and talk to her about boy problems.

I wanted her to pull me into a hug and tell me that everything was going to be okay. That everyone goes through this kind of pain with their first love.

And I wanted her to make me cookies and watch romantic movies with me while I cried my eyes out.

But none of that was going to happen.

She was sick, and I needed to be that support for her.

Feeling incredibly selfish, I unbuckled and pulled open the car door. Mom was probably sleeping, and knowing Dad and Paul, the house was a mess. I owed it to Mom to help out, and if I didn't get cleaning now, I would be too tired and would have to face the mess tomorrow.

I kicked off my shoes in the entryway of the house. The only light on the first floor of the house was light that came from a small lamp that we'd found and plugged in the first night we got here.

Boxes still littered the floor and cast shadows on the ground in front of me, only intensifying my guilt. Dad was busy with work and Paul was busy with what he was doing. If this house was going to get unpacked, it was up to me to do it.

I shuffled into the kitchen and started tackling the dishes. Thankfully, from the leftover pizza boxes and sauce smeared plates, they had takeout. Which meant there were less dishes to do.

I yawned as I worked. Tired of the silence, I turned on some music to keep me awake. I felt accomplished as I wiped down the countertops to the sound of the dishwasher humming behind me. My energy had returned, so I moved to grab a pair of scissors and cut the tape of a nearby box. Most of the kitchen was still packed, so I figured I'd start here.

I was so lost in the music and unpacking that I barely heard the doorbell ring. At first, I thought it was from the song, but when it came again, I reached over and turned down the music. Realizing that someone was at the door, I set down the bowl that I'd just been unwrapping and moved to the front of the house.

"Yes—"

I stopped when I pulled open the door and saw Blake standing in front of me. The left side of his face was bloodied and swollen, and he had a look of desperation in his eyes. I blinked, wondering for a moment if I was dreaming.

"Blake?" I asked, stepping toward him as if there was something I could do right now. I had no towel. No gauze. Nothing to stop the slow drip of blood that was rolling down his cheek.

"Can I come in?"

I swallowed as all words left my mind. Instead of asking, I stepped out of the way and waved him in. "Of course."

11

SUSIE

Blake didn't wait for another invitation. He was inside of my house in a matter of seconds.

"Thanks."

I nodded and glanced outside for a moment, wondering who did this to him. Then, realizing that I wasn't that formidable at five foot four and weaponless, I quickly made my way inside and shut the door.

Blake was standing in the middle of the entryway and looked as lost as I felt. I stood there with my hands in front of me, wanting to ask what happened but knowing that it wasn't really any of my business.

"Do you want me to get Paul?" I finally asked. After all, as much as I wanted to think that he was here to see me, I knew better. Something probably happened, and he needed to crash at his buddy's house until things calmed down.

As much as I wanted to be part of this equation, I knew that wasn't a reality.

Blake glanced up the stairs and then back down at me. I could see that he was conflicted. "Is he sleeping?"

I shrugged and moved to walk up the stairs. "I can go check." As soon as I hit the first step, a hand reached out and wrapped around my arm.

"It's okay. I don't want to bother him if he is."

Warmth was radiating up my arm from where Blake was holding onto me. I stopped and turned to see him staring at me. My breath caught in my throat. Despite the swollen, bloodiness that was his cut, I could feel his intensity as he studied me.

"Think you could help me?" he asked. His voice had turned husky, and the air around us was palpable. He had to feel this.

Right?

I swallowed, my throat drying up. "Sure," I managed out. Luckily, I'd just unpacked our first aid kit earlier.

Blake didn't move to drop his hand right away. Instead, it lingered on my arm for what felt like a moment longer than necessary. I didn't mind, of course. If anything, I wanted to lean into it.

He eventually let go, and I took that moment to get some space between us. I motioned toward the kitchen. "Follow me."

I led him around the assorted boxes that I'd opened and to the powder room on the other side. He sat down on the closed toilet while I got the kit from under the sink. I could feel him watching me as I dug around inside looking for antibiotic cream and bandages.

"Aren't you going to ask me?" he finally asked, breaking the silence and startling me so that I instantly looked over at him.

"Hmm?" I asked. I'd found what I needed and moved to turn on the warm water.

"You haven't asked me what happened."

He was so direct that I wasn't sure what I was supposed to do with what he said. "Do you want me to know what happened to you?" I asked.

He quirked an eyebrow but then winced and hunched over from the pain. "Most people ask if I show up on their doorstep with a bloodied face."

"Most people?" Was he saying that he did this on the regular? "Does this happen a lot?" The gauze that I was currently running under the water was sufficiently wet, so I squeezed it out and moved closer to him.

The temperature around me instantly rose as I stood inches from his face. His gaze never left me. "Most people who care about others ask."

I paused, dropping my gaze down to meet his. What did he mean by this? Did he want me to care? How much? And in what way?

"I care," I whispered before I could stop myself. Before I could mull over the words I'd just spoken.

"You do?"

This conversation was getting confusing. I needed to guide it in the direction that made sense. "Like I care about all my friends." There. I was going to establish boundaries if he wasn't. I knew he'd never care for me like I wanted him to, so I might as well make sure that he knew where I was comfortable enough to stand.

Blake was silent for a moment before he said, "Friends."

I leaned forward and began dabbing his forehead with the gauze. "Yes, friends. Well, you could say fake boyfriend and girlfriend." I pulled back enough to shrug. "But Hannah's not around, so no need for labels."

Blake didn't say anything. Instead, he just studied me as I cleaned up his cut. He had a gash down his eyebrow that had created all of the blood, but thankfully, it was already starting to clot which made clean up easier.

Once I'd washed off all the blood, I threw away the soiled gauze. Just as I turned back with the antibiotic cream in hand, Blake startled me. He was closer to me now, and his gaze was much more earnest than before.

"Is that all you see me as?" he asked.

I blinked, not sure where he was going with this. "What do you mean?"

"Am I just a fake boyfriend to you?"

I swallowed. Did he really want to know? Or did I really want to tell him? "Yes," I said, but my shallow voice and my pounding heart were sure giveaways that I didn't mean a word of what I was saying.

Blake slowly rose from his seat until he was towering over me. I could feel his warmth cascading over me even though we weren't touching. His gaze held mine as he stared at me. "Really?"

Why did my cheeks betray me like they were? Why was my heart pounding like a jack hammer in my chest? Why couldn't I stop looking at his lips and wondering what they would feel like against my own?

Why couldn't we just be friends and fake boyfriend and girlfriend and leave it at that?

"Blake," I whispered. I needed him to stop doing this. I was already falling for him. Why did he want more from me? After all, he wanted Hannah, and last I checked, I wasn't Hannah.

He leaned closer. I wanted to believe it was because he wanted to kiss me. But I feared it was just to hear what I was saying because I could barely hear what I was saying.

"What do you want, Susie?" His gaze was earnest. Like he really wanted to know.

I parted my lips to speak. I wanted to tell him; I did. But I wasn't sure how. Or what he would say once my secret was out in the open.

And to be honest, I feared how I would feel once I heard my secret escape my lips. The truth that I was pretending didn't exist. The truth that I wanted him. All of him.

"I want…" I paused, gathering what courage I had left.

My heart was so broken, and yet, it was as if I were a glutton for punishment. Mom was sick, and I was moments away from creating a broken heart for myself.

"...to put a bandage on your cut."

The grip fear had on me was too strong. I couldn't just tell him that I liked him. Not when we had a plan. Not when I was so close to breaking that one tap would cause me to crumble. I had to stay intact for Mom. She deserved a complete Susie.

Blake furrowed his brow. If moving his eyebrows hurt, he didn't move to show it. Instead, he studied me for a moment before he plopped down on the toilet and said, "Then go ahead."

Thankful that the tension in the room dissipated slightly, I hurried to wipe the cream on his cut and then place a bandage over it. It was hard, but I think I managed to avoid getting any of his eyebrows in the bandage tape.

Once I was finished, I took a big step back. I doubted I would be able to last much longer being this close to him. My strength to resist him was only so strong. Keeping my distance was the only thing to keep me sane.

Blake was hard to read as he paused for a moment before he stood. He pushed his hand through his hair as he turned to inspect my work in the mirror. I wasn't sure what to do, so I lingered in the shadows.

"Thanks," he mumbled as he turned to look at me. He leaned against the sink and rested his hands on either side of him.

"Of course. If I can help, I'm here." I shrugged and offered him a small smile.

"I'm getting that." His tone was deep, and I could feel his appreciation in his gaze and voice.

I kept my smile going as I glanced around. Blake wasn't running out of here, so I wasn't sure what to do. "Are you hungry?"

He studied me. "I don't want to be a bother."

I shook my head. "No bother. I'm sure I can find something."

Blake nodded. "Okay."

We exited the bathroom. Blake settled down on one of the barstools and then spun so that he was facing me. I walked over to the fridge and pulled open the door. Thankfully, someone in my family had enough forethought to put away the pizza that they'd eaten. I grabbed the plastic bag and set it on the counter. "Pizza?" I asked.

Blake shrugged. "Sounds good."

I focused my attention on warming up the pizza. Once the microwave was on and the plate was rotating, I moved to grab a root beer from the fridge. I popped the top and handed it over to Blake.

"Thanks."

Things were so quiet in the room that I wasn't sure what to say. I wanted things to be normal between us. At least, for Blake to be normal around me. I feared that he suspected that I had feelings for him which was why things had become awkward between us.

The microwave beeped, so I opened it and pulled out the pizza. Blake started devouring it as soon as I put it in front of him. Not wanting to stand there and watch him eat his pizza, I moved to unpack the box that I'd been working on.

The sound of the faucet turning on drew my attention over. Blake rinsed his plate and then pulled open the dishwasher and loaded it. I couldn't help but smile. Everything he did just made him better and better.

"That was delicious," Blake said as he turned the water off and then leaned against the counter. He didn't look like he had any intention of leaving which made me wonder if his dad had been the reason his eye was currently swollen.

"Thanks. It was here when I got home." I unwrapped a plate and then turned and slipped it on top of the stack I'd started.

"Your family knows how to order some interesting toppings." Blake's voice came closer to me, and suddenly, his arm appeared as he set a plate on top of the stack.

I smiled at his comment. Mom always tried to spice things up and try different combinations. Some were great. Some, not so much. "Yeah, that's mom. She said she wants to experience everything before…" My voice trailed off when I realized where I was going with this comment.

What was I going to say? Before she dies? Before she's gone? Before I was going to be left without a mom?

A sob escaped my lips before I could stop it. Tears

formed in my eyes, and I blinked hard to keep them from escaping. I covered my mouth with my hand, praying that I could gather myself enough to move forward.

Blake's arms appeared on either side of me, and suddenly, I was being pulled to his chest. I didn't fight him. If anything, I welcomed it. As soon as I collapsed against his chest, I let my tears flow.

I was hurting. Hurting that Mom was sick. Hurting because I couldn't help her. And hurting for the future Susie who might have to navigate her life without her mother.

Blake just held me while I cried. I wasn't sure how long I stood there, sobbing into his shirt, but when I pulled away, I cringed when I saw the water ring on his shirt.

"I'm so sorry," I whispered as I reached up and tried to wipe away some of the moisture. Which was ridiculous. There was nothing that could fix this problem.

Blake shrugged. "I'll be fine. It'll dry."

I sighed as I pulled away and folded my arms across my chest. Blake reached over and grabbed a paper towel and handed it to me. "Feel better?"

I hated that I was blubbering and that he was currently watching me wipe my nose. It made me feel like such a loser to break down like that. But the truth was, I felt great. Standing there, wrapped in Blake's arms, my life didn't seem so crappy.

I felt less alone.

"Yeah," I whispered as I folded the paper towel in half and wiped my nose again.

"I got into a fight with my dad."

I paused, staring down at my paper towel as I let his words settle around me. It had been what I'd expected; it was just strange to hear them spoken out loud. I slowly raised my gaze up to study him.

Blake's arms were folded, and his jaw was clenched. He was staring hard at the ground as if those words were hard to speak and he was just now processing that information.

"I'm so sorry," I whispered. I wished I had something better to say. After all, he'd been there for me. I felt better having him around. I couldn't help but fear that with my weak condolences and my lack of movement toward comforting him, I would come across as a bad friend.

Which I wasn't. I wanted to hug him like he'd hugged me. But I didn't know how, and I wasn't sure if what he told me should be met with the same amount of physical affection as what I was going through with Mom.

Blake pushed his hand through his hair and shrugged. "I'm used to it."

I shook my head. I may not feel comfortable hugging him, but I wasn't going to allow him to stand there and think that he deserved what happened. "That's not something you should get used to."

Blake's gaze snapped over to me, and I felt like I was

going to melt under his stare. It was so intense that it physically took my breath away. Then he sighed and shrugged.

"Yeah, well. Things at home aren't great. You could probably tell that."

I shook my head, hating that I was lying to him. The honest answer was I could tell. But I didn't want him to think that his struggles were out there for people to see. After all, I knew what that was like. I hated when people knew about Mom. It always changed our relationship dynamics.

"Anything I can do to help?"

Blake shifted his weight, his gaze dropping to the ground. "Can I stay here?"

I blinked, surprised by his question. "You want to stay here?"

His gaze returned to mine, and I could see the pain there. He was hurting, and I wanted to take it away. It was strange that he was asking my permission. That felt like something he should ask Paul.

"I think that'll be okay." I wrapped my arms around my chest and nodded. I knew Mom wouldn't object and Dad already considered him another son. Paul would be thrilled to have him stay, so why was Blake reacting like he was stepping over boundaries?

"I just figured with your rules, this might be breaking one of them." He shoved his hands into his front pockets, and his flirty, teasing smile emerged.

I scoffed and rolled my eyes. Of course, he would take

this moment when we were feeling vulnerable and make a joke at my expense. "Hey, my rules are keeping us sane."

He held my gaze and then nodded. "Okay." Before I could respond, he glanced around. "So, I guess I better head upstairs and find out what Paul's up to."

"Unless you want to stay in my room." The words were out before I could stop myself.

Blake seemed equally surprised when he turned to look at me. "Um, what?" he asked, leaning closer to me as if he wanted to make sure that he heard every word.

"Nothing," I whispered, pinching my lips.

"You want me to stay in your room?" He sucked in his breath. "Isn't that a violation of all of your rules?"

I wanted to point out that staying in my room technically didn't break any of my rules. His presence there didn't mean that we needed to flirt, kiss, or even look at each other. But I feared that response might be mistaken as me trying to convince him, so I just shrugged.

"I was just being hospitable."

He pulled back, but the smile on his lips and the look on his face told me that he didn't believe me at all. "Okay," he said, his words taking a *sure you are* tone. Then he leaned forward. "You keep telling me to follow the rules, but you're over here, breaking them all yourself."

I glowered at him, but he didn't wait around to hear my reply. Instead, he grinned and pulled back, then turned to jog toward the stairs. I parted my lips to respond, but nothing came out. Instead, I just stood there, looking like a fool.

Blake was gone by the time my head was finally on straight. I sighed as I leaned against the counter, suddenly feeling exhausted. With school in the morning, I needed to get to sleep, or I was never going to be able to wake up.

My body was dragging by the time I crawled into bed. Blake never resurfaced, so I figured Paul had agreed to take care of him. As I lay there, tucked under my blankets, I let my mind wander.

Sleep evaded me as I thought back to my evening with Blake. The feeling I got when I was with him. The warmth that spread throughout my entire body as he wrapped his arms around me. Or the fact that I felt comfortable enough around him to both cry and laugh in the same span of time.

One thing was for sure; this was no longer fake.

Not even a little.

12

SUSIE

The smell of bacon and eggs wafted into my room the next morning. I groaned and stretched out on the bed, taking in a deep breath which activated my salivary glands. I smacked my lips as I fought the desire to get up with the desire to stay in bed.

Then realizing that I was going to have to go to school, I groaned and rolled off my bed. I dressed quickly, pulled a brush through my hair, and threw it up into a ponytail. I felt somewhat normal as I grabbed my backpack and hurried down the stairs.

Mom was standing in the kitchen with a deep purple bandana wrapped around her head. She was slowly sipping on a mug, and I could tell from the way her eyes crinkled, she was smiling.

As soon as she saw me, she set her mug down and walked over to me. We hugged, and when I pulled back, I glanced in the direction that she had been looking when I walked in to find Blake standing next to the stove with an apron on and a spatula in his hand.

He was studying me, and when our gazes met, he smiled before dropping his attention back to the stove.

"Did you sleep well?" Mom asked, drawing my gaze over to her.

I nodded. "Yeah." Sure, that was a lie. Truth was, I spent half my night trying to decipher Blake's actions and the other half, getting angry with myself for not sleeping.

Luckily, the bags under my eyes weren't too bad, and my foundation was doing a good enough job at masking what I did have.

Mom was studying me when I drew my focus back to her. She looked like a detective as she stood there, eyeing me. I shot her a smile before I side stepped her and headed over to the fridge.

"Don't get any food out. I've got some food for you."

I glanced over to Blake to see him wave a spatula in my direction. I nodded and then turned back to the fridge and grabbed out the orange juice. After I filled up a glass, I turned to lean against the counter and sipped slowly, trying to keep my gaze from wandering over to Blake.

"Can you believe what happened to Blake's face?" Mom's voice was one of disbelief as she waved in Blake's direction.

I glanced at him and then over to Mom. Did he tell her?

"I don't know what got into Honey. She's normally so docile."

I paused. Honey?

"You be careful on horses, Susie."

I couldn't help but stare at Blake. He was blaming his horse for what happened?

Before I could respond, Paul entered the kitchen. He had a ball cap on his head and his backpack slung over his shoulder. He didn't acknowledge us as he barreled into the room and then plopped down on the nearest chair. He stretched out his leg and leaned against the chair.

Once it seemed as if he wasn't going to say or do anything, everyone in the room went back to focusing on whatever task they were doing. I had my orange juice, Blake was flipping bacon, and Mom was sipping on her coffee once more.

"It's so nice that you stayed the night," Mom said, breaking the silence.

Blake turned and grinned. "I'm happy you guys were so hospitable." As he turned back to the stove, his gaze landed on me once more. His smile faltered as his expression became more intense.

My breath caught in my throat, and I felt so overwhelmed that I dropped my gaze. Whatever was happening between us needed to stop. I needed to not care for Blake. Despite the fact that he'd opened up to me last night about his dad or that he let me cry tear stains onto his shirt. He wasn't interested in me like that even *if* I wanted him to be.

Which I didn't.

Or at least, I spent the greater part of last night trying to convince myself that I didn't.

Feeling frustrated and losing my appetite, I moved to dump my remaining orange juice down the sink and then moved to shoulder my backpack. I knew Blake wanted me to eat his breakfast, but I needed to get out of the house.

I needed some fresh air.

I gave Mom a quick kiss on the cheek as I passed by her to the back door.

"Where are you going?" Blake called after me.

I tossed a quick smile over my shoulder. "I've got to get to school."

"What about—"

The door was shut behind me before he could finish. Anger began to brew inside of my gut. Why did Blake want me around him so much? After all, if he was desperate to get Hannah back, he needed to hang around Hannah.

Did he just want me around so that he could feel better about himself? I was fairly certain that I was not good at hiding my feelings for him. Did he pick up on them? Is that why he wanted to hang out with me?

Here I was, this idiot, who thought that we'd grown closer. That perhaps, we could be more than friends. But I was wrong. At the end of the day, he wanted Hannah.

I was not Hannah.

I blew out my breath as I tipped my face toward the sky. The sunlight beat down on me. The sound of gravel crunched beneath my shoes. I wasn't sure what I was going to do—school was a ten-minute drive from my house. All I knew was that I couldn't be in the same room as Blake for a moment longer.

I was about a half a mile down the road when I heard the sound of wheels on the dirt road coming up from behind me. I quickly made my way to the grass that grew alongside the road to let it pass. When it didn't move, I glanced over my shoulder and sighed.

Blake was behind the wheel of his truck, giving me a small smile.

I forced a return smile and gave him a quick wave. The universal sign for, you can go. Blake didn't move to drive past me. Instead, he stopped, and suddenly, the driver's door was flung open.

His feet were on the ground before I could run. He crossed the space between us in three long strides. His look of determination wavered the closer he got. By the time he was towering over me, he looked nervous.

"Where are you going?" he finally asked after what felt like an eternity.

I swallowed, hating that his presence made me feel this way, and then waved in the direction that I'd been heading. "School."

His gaze followed my gesture until he was squinting as

he stared down the road. "Do you normally walk to school?"

"No," I finally squeaked out. Blake raised his eyebrows as if he were expecting me to continue. Not sure what to say, I just shrugged. "It sounded nice today."

Lies. It was all lies. I was running away from him. I hated how much he had infiltrated my life and my mind. I needed to remain sane, but being around him as much as I was, hampered that resolution.

"Why don't you get in my truck, and I'll give you a ride?" He waved toward his truck as if that was all it was going to take to convince me to accept.

I looped my thumbs behind the shoulder straps of my backpack. "I think I'll stick to walking."

His eyebrows went up again. "Susie, I—"

"Listen, we made the rules, and I think we should stick to them." I gathered my courage and turned my gaze to meet his head on. I hated how confused he looked. Like he wasn't sure why I was acting this way. But I needed to remain strong. I needed to set boundaries, or I was scared that I might just lose my heart.

Blake was quiet for a moment before he scoffed and nodded. "Rules, right," he muttered under his breath.

"I'm going to text Patty to see if she can pick me up. You head back to my house and finish hanging out with my mom." My stomach squeezed at the mention of her. She seemed so happy this morning, and I hated that I ran out on her. I was missing valuable time with her just to avoid Blake.

I was stupid and let myself fall for him. Had I been stronger, I wouldn't be in the predicament that I found myself in now. That thought only made me more determined to distance myself from Blake. To remain strong so that I could be there for Mom when she needed me the most.

"Susie, I'm not sure..." His voice trailed off as he studied me. His gaze raked my face as if he were waiting for a signal or a sign that I might want something different.

Even though I did. Even though I wanted him here with me. I wanted to return to my house with him by my side. I wanted his strength to make up for when mine was lacking; I couldn't give into that want.

I needed to draw a line and force myself to never cross it.

He shoved his hand through his hair and then nodded. "If that's what you want."

I nodded even though every part of me wanted to scream, *no!*

Blake lingered for a moment before he turned and headed to his truck. He got into the driver's seat and let the engine idle. His gaze was suddenly on me with an intensity that took my breath away. I gave him a small smile as I held up my phone and then moved to text Patty.

Me: Wanna pick me up? I'm currently walking to school, and I'm at the Bruster's Barn.

I sent that off and then slipped my phone into my back pocket. Blake still lingered by me, and I began to fear that he was going to wait until Patty got here before he left. I let out my breath when he pulled away from the side of the road, u-turned, and then headed back the direction he'd come.

I watched his truck as it grew smaller and smaller, turned right, and disappeared. Feeling exhausted, I collapsed in the grass, bringing my knees to my chest and resting my chin there.

Patty texted a thumbs up emoji, and ten minutes later, she pulled up next to me. I stood and pulled open the passenger door.

"Good morning," Patty sang out.

I could only muster a weak smile.

"Oh. You look like you have a story to tell," she said as she put the car into drive and started down the road.

I moaned and leaned my head against the head rest behind me. "I'm in trouble," I whispered.

If Patty heard me, she didn't move to say anything, which told me Patty didn't hear me. Instead, she told me about her morning as if she picked up on the fact that I really wasn't in the mood to talk.

I wanted to praise my best friend for being so amazing. But that would only draw attention to the fact that I was having a problem which would only force me to feel guilty that I wasn't telling her, so I remained quiet and let her talk.

She pulled into the school parking lot, and we headed into the school. We were early which I was grateful for. A few students were sitting at the cafeteria tables as we walked by. Patty had moved to tell me about her evening last night, and I was finally feeling relaxed enough, just listening to her words.

We got to her locker, and she turned. "Okay. I was patient enough. Spill." She narrowed her eyes as she stared at me. "Does this have to do with Blake?"

I parted my lips as I got ready to tell her that it wasn't. I wanted to draw her attention away from him. I knew she didn't like him, and the last thing I needed was for her to tell me, *I told you so.*

She didn't wait for my answer as she turned to do the combination of her locker. "Blake Marshall is a player," she said as she pulled open her locker.

Great. My feelings betrayed me and must have been written all over my face. One look and she knew exactly what was wrong with me. Realizing that it was pointless to try to hide my feelings, I moved to collapse against the locker next to hers. "He is," I whispered.

Patty shuffled some books around from her locker to her backpack and then slammed the door. "I watched him break Corinne's heart." She was holding her books to her chest, and a sad expression passed over her face.

"Corinne?"

She nodded. "She was my best friend last year. She took a job at the dude ranch where they worked. He was all flirty with her. He spent a lot of time with her. Took her horseback riding. They even kissed..."

I winced at her words. This was starting to sound familiar—minus the kiss part. Was this a pattern for him? Was I just another notch on his belt? To be fair, this was supposed to be fake, and I was the one who was having troubles keeping it that way. But still, this wasn't painting him in a good light.

"Then suddenly, he dropped her. No explanation as to why. Just told her that they couldn't be anything and then walked away." Patty's eyes narrowed. "She was devastated."

"What happened to her?" In all the time that I'd known Patty, she never mentioned a Corinne.

"Her family moved to Japan at the end of the summer."

"Because of Blake?"

Patty looked at me strange. "No. Because of her dad's job. But she was ready to go. We tried to talk long distance, but she told me that I just reminded her of Glories Bluff and it was too hard to be friends in different time zones. So, we just stopped talking." Her expression morphed into one of sadness.

"Oh, Patty, I'm so sorry," I said as I reached out and wrapped an arm around her.

She was quiet for a moment before she shrugged. "It's okay. I've got you now."

We made our way back into the cafeteria and over to

an empty table. I collapsed on one of the chairs while Patty wandered over to the food and picked up something for us to eat. Students started arriving in thicker and thicker crowds, but we really weren't paying attention as we sat and ate and talked.

It wasn't until Patty was staring over my head that I realized that someone was behind me.

Turning, my heart stopped in my tracks when I saw that it was Blake. He was staring down at me with a perturbed look. Not sure what to do but realizing that he wasn't going to leave until I spoke to him, I stood.

"Hey," I said after he led me a few feet away from the table.

"You didn't text me." He was staring off to the side. His jaw muscles were twitching as if he were angry with me.

"I'm sorry. Why did I need to text you?" I tucked my hair behind my ear. I hated that he seemed so bothered, but I needed to create boundaries if I was going to survive this school year—and honestly, life in general.

He glanced over at me. "You could have told me that you got to school safe. I spent most of the morning worried that you had been kidnapped."

Guilt flooded my stomach. "Oh, that. Sorry." That thought hadn't even crossed my mind. Probably because I was making a concerted effort *not* to think about him.

Blake's expression softened, and he stepped forward. I braced myself for what he was going to do, but he never moved to touch me. Instead, he paused and then stepped back. "Are we okay?"

My mouth went dry. I swallowed hard, hoping that was all it would take to wet it and nodded. "Yeah, we're cool."

He narrowed his eyes but then sighed. "You're just acting strange, that's all."

The truth was, I wanted Blake. I wanted to be his friend. I wanted to be more. But I knew what I was getting into when I agreed to this. I knew that this was all fake, especially to him.

From what I'd heard from Patty, he was a player—but I already knew that.

"I think we just need to remember why we are doing this whole fake relationship thing and keep to our resolve." I gave him a weak smile.

He studied me. "You do?"

I nodded. "It's for the best. You'll have Hannah, and I'll get back to my normal life."

He furrowed his brow. "You want me to have Hannah?"

His stare was intense. As if he were daring me to say something different. "That's what we agreed to. I'd help you get Hannah, like Mom wanted."

He was quiet for a moment. "Is that what you want?"

No. It wasn't. It was going to break my heart watching him hang out with another girl knowing I helped them get back together. But I'd rather knowingly have my heart broken than have the rug pulled out from underneath me. And that was going to happen if I allowed myself to fall for him like I was quickly doing.

"Yes," was all I could whisper. I held his gaze in my sad attempt to hold my ground.

He studied my gaze for a moment before he sighed. "Okay."

He shouldered his backpack and turned to walk away. I watched him retreat for a moment before I dropped my gaze and hurried over to Patty. She was sitting at the table, watching our interaction.

"Everything okay?"

I wanted to break down and cry. I wanted to tell her that my heart was broken and I doubted that it would ever heal. But I knew she didn't want to hear that, and there was no way that I wanted to put that vulnerability out into the air. So, I just forced a smile and nodded.

"It's perfect."

13

SUSIE

Blake stuck to my request the rest of the week at school. He kept his flirting to a bare minimum and only when Hannah was around—much to my happiness and chagrin. After all, I liked when he joked with me, and I missed it. Flirtless Blake was a little bland. A little boring.

But our plan seemed to be working.

There were a few times that I turned the corner on my way to class only to find Hannah standing dangerously close to Blake. They were laughing and joking, and every time, a slice of jealousy would rip through my gut.

Hannah would barely acknowledge me. Instead, she would keep her close proximity and even go so far as to lay her hand on his arm. The way she would bat her eyelashes up at him made me want to vomit.

Blake was a great actor and was excellent at keeping

up the *I'm dating Susie* routine and would move to push her away and walk up to me. The eye daggers she would throw my way were so intense that I feared for my life.

On Friday, I swear I saw steam coming from her ears as Blake dragged me away from where she was standing and around the corner, so I was no longer in her line of sight.

"We've got to come up with a plan because I'm worried that I'm going to find her standing over my bed with a knife in hand ready to end me," I whispered as I leaned against the wall, letting the cool feeling of the brick seep through my shirt. It took a few days, but I managed to push my feelings down enough to focus on this task. Mom was eating up my stories, and Blake and Hannah seemed as if they were moments away from making up, which meant I was almost done with this torturous plot.

And I needed it to be done.

Blake was standing in front of me, studying me as I spoke.

It wasn't until I straightened that I realized how close we were. My heart took off racing and I wondered…could he hear it? I mentally shook that thought from my mind and focused on how earnest Blake looked.

"What?" I asked, slowly.

His expression turned pleading. "I have a favor to ask."

I hugged the books I'd been holding closer to my chest. I wasn't sure I liked the sound of this. "Okay," I said suspiciously.

He swallowed which made his Adam's apple rise and fall. His reaction was making me nervous. What was he going to ask?

"Is there any way that you'd want to come with me to a party tonight?" he asked.

I felt my resolve to keep him at arm's length dissolving around me. He looked so panicked, so nervous, it made me wonder why. Was he scared of me? Of what I might say? Did his relationship with Hannah matter that much?

I wasn't sure how I felt about that, so I pushed that question to the far corners of my mind and focused on what he was asking me. "Tonight?"

He nodded.

I wanted to say yes, but just as I parted my lips to speak, I remembered that Patty and I were going to hang out at the house with Mom. Ever since Patty told me about her history with Blake and I'd reassured her over and over that I would never do that, she seemed more relaxed around us. She was even okay with Blake sitting at our lunch table.

But if I ditched her to hang out with Blake, I was worried what that might do to our friendship and the reassurances that I'd made to her.

"Please?" His eyes widened and somehow grew bigger. It was as if I were staring into the eyes of a cartoon cat who wanted to eat my food.

I sighed. What kind of fake girlfriend would I be if I didn't say yes? Besides, with the way Hannah had been hanging on him earlier, their reconciliation wasn't far away. If I went with him to this party, then he could hook up with Hannah and my job would be over.

I could focus on Mom and Patty and get over my ridiculous crush on my brother's best friend.

It seemed like a win/win for everyone—even if my heart felt as if it were breaking as I thought those words.

"Fine," I said, and suddenly, I was airborne.

Blake had wrapped his arms around me and pulled me off the ground into a crushing hug. He pinned my arms to my books and my books to my chest. The air in my lungs came whooshing out, but that wasn't what I was focusing on. Instead, all I could think about was how good he smelled and how he lifted me like I weighed nothing at all.

Or how his heart was pounding similar to mine as he held me close.

All of my will to keep away from him washed away, and I suddenly wanted this to be real. I wanted him to want to hold me like this.

I wanted him to feel as unsure and nervous as I did.

"Put me down," I whispered.

My feet were planted on the ground as quickly as they'd turned airborne. Blake took a step back. "Sorry," he muttered as he pushed his hand through his hair. "I get a little carried away sometimes."

I shook my head. "It's okay." Then I studied him, trying to figure out why he was so excited to go to this party. "What's the plan tonight?"

He glanced up at me. "I'll pick you up at seven, and we can head on over."

I waited to see if he was going to add anything more. "And?"

"And?" He furrowed his brow.

"And once we get there, what's the plan?"

His lips formed an o shape and he nodded. "Oh, Hannah's ready to talk." He looked sheepish as he shoved his hands into the front pockets of his jeans like he wasn't supposed to tell me that.

"That's awesome," I managed to get out over the sharp pain that filled my chest. My head was telling me that it was awesome, but my heart seemed to think differently. "So, are we going to stage a big breakup scene?" I asked.

I was kind of ready for all of this to end. I wanted to move on from Blake. As much as I'd loved hanging out with him and getting to know him on so many different levels, it made my head spin, and I was ready to be a single gal once more. Mom's little experiment was over, and I was ready to put it in my rearview mirror.

Hopefully, I could find a way to get over Blake. I'd convinced myself that all it was going to take was to see Blake with Hannah to make myself realize that I was never going to have him. That we were never going to have the relationship that I wanted.

I was ready to have my heart broken by Blake now, before it was too late.

The bell for the next class rang. Grateful for my exit, I

told Blake I'd be ready at seven, and then I hurried to class. My stomach was in knots the rest of the day. I barely ate anything at lunch, and my mind was in a fog for every class. Thankfully, it was the end of the week, and it seemed as if my teachers felt that too. They gave minimal lectures and allowed us to spend most of our time catching up on homework.

Once school was out, I hurried to find Patty. She was coming over, and we were going to bake cookies with Mom. I swear, Mom was growing to love Patty more than me. She'd come over every day this week, and those two would laugh and gossip like two old ladies.

I loved it, listening to them. It made Mom seem more alive. More vibrant. There were times when I even forgot that she was sick. And then that memory would come rushing back to me at random times, and I would have to fight the urge to cry.

How many more days did I have with Mom like this?

When Patty and I walked into the kitchen after the drive home, Mom was nowhere to be found. The two sticks of butter that I'd put out on the counter were still there, but nothing else. Patty moved to the fridge where she pulled out a bottle of water. We'd managed to unpack most of the first floor now, so the house was starting to feel like home.

"Let me go see if I can find where she is," I said over my shoulder as I moved to the living room.

I finally found Mom curled up in bed. Her drapes

were drawn shut and her fan was set to high. Her cue for, *I'm in pain and I need to sleep.*

Feeling defeated, I pulled her door shut and tiptoed back downstairs.

"Everything okay?" Patty asked.

I shrugged, fighting the urge to break down. Instead, I found a bottle of water for myself and cracked the lid. "She's sleeping."

Patty glanced in the direction of the stairs and nodded. "Oh." Then she sighed. "So, what do you want to do?"

Needing some time to relax before my plans with Blake later tonight, I stretched out and nodded toward the living room. "Wanna watch a movie?" I needed something mind numbing for the next few hours.

We settled on an old romantic comedy which seemed to be exactly what I needed. After it was finished, Patty glanced at her phone and declared that she should get home. She'd agreed to babysit her neighbor's kids, so the parents could go on a date.

I gave her a smile as I walked her to the front door. I was actually glad she was leaving. I wanted to get ready for this party alone. Even though things that involved Blake seemed to have settled, I didn't want to remind her of her history.

I shut the door and then turned and leaned against it. I rested my head behind me as I closed my eyes. I let out a big sigh and pinched the bridge of my nose. Was I ready for my fake relationship with Blake to end?

No. If I were truly honest with myself, I still wanted Blake all to myself. I wanted our relationship to mean something to him.

I wanted him to break up with Hannah and choose me.

But that was a pipe dream. Plus, I'd agreed to make this all fake. I wasn't in the business of changing my mind either.

Despite deciding that my feelings for Blake didn't matter, I spent the better part of an hour getting ready. I showered, got dressed, and focused longer than I wanted to admit on my makeup.

By the time seven rolled around, I looked amazing. I'd completely transformed myself, and it was shocking even to myself. I stared at my reflection, both excited and scared of what Blake would think.

Would he realize that I cared for him like I did? It was obvious that I was trying to impress someone, but would Blake know it was him? I swallowed against the lump in my throat as tears once more began to form in my eyes. I blinked rapidly in an effort to push them back.

The last thing I needed was to cry and undo everything that I'd worked so hard to do.

Thankfully, the doorbell rang. I welcomed the distraction as I grabbed my purse and hurried downstairs.

In all of my preparation, nothing could have prepared me for the look on Blake's face when I opened the door. His eyes were wide as he stared at me.

"Susie?" he asked, his voice so low that I almost didn't hear it. "You look amazing." His eyes widened as if he suddenly heard what he said, but he never moved to take it back. Like it was the truth, and he wasn't ashamed that he'd said it.

My heart pounded from his words, and my body felt light. I hated how much I loved the way he looked at me and the way he appreciated what he saw. It made me feel things that I'd never felt in my life.

It made me feel...alive.

"Thanks," I said, feeling antsy that I was just standing there while he stared at me. Ready to get on with the evening, I stepped out onto the stoop and shut the front door behind me.

It seemed like a good idea in my head, but in reality, that move had been a mistake. Suddenly, I was standing extremely close to Blake. When I'd calculated the move, I'd expected Blake to step back when he saw me moving toward him...but he didn't. Instead, he seemed rooted to his spot, and I was now centimeters from him.

Unsure of what to do, but unable to keep from looking at him, I slowly raised my gaze up to find his. He was towering over me, and his gaze felt hot as it combined with mine. There was so much to unpack in his expression that it scared me.

I wanted Blake to like me. I wanted to know that every time my heart pounded, his did as well.

He wants Hannah.

Those three words snapped me out of my trance. I blinked and then stepped back. "Are you ready?" I asked, thankful that I had enough strength to speak.

Blake furrowed his brow and just when I thought he was going to speak, he just nodded, turned, and bounded down the steps.

With him gone, I felt as if I could breathe again. I tipped my head up toward the sky for a moment and filled my lungs.

I could do this—I could. Once this evening was over, my life would return to normal. My focus would be on Mom, and what I felt for Blake would be a distant memory.

I just needed to get through tonight which, after my moment with Blake, felt easier said than done.

14

SUSIE

Music was blaring from the open windows when Blake pulled up to the house. I peered out the window at the people milling about on the grass. We were a good distance from the road and any other houses. I wondered how many complaints parties in Montana got since there was no one around to be bothered by the noise.

Blake pulled his truck off onto the grass and parked it next to another truck. Actually, when I really took it in, every vehicle here was a truck.

Only in the country.

"Ready?" Blake asked.

I turned to see him studying me. Not sure what to say, I just nodded. "Yep."

I was ready to get this evening over with and to start my new life, sans Blake.

He turned off the engine and opened his door. I

followed suit, jumping down onto the grass. Blake was fast, rounding the hood of his truck and stepping up next to me before I could even process what was going on.

He smiled down at me, and I took in a deep breath. I could do this.

We walked a few feet toward the house when I felt Blake step closer to me. My breath caught in my throat as I waited for what he was going to do.

"Can I hold your hand?" His tone was soft, and I swear I could feel his warmth as he stood so close to me; we might as well have been touching.

"What?" I asked, just to make sure that I'd heard him right. I turned to see him staring down at me.

"I think it'll be more believable if we are holding hands."

"More believable?"

"That we are dating."

"Right."

I flexed my fingers as the desire to hold his hand rose up inside of me. Was I strong enough to let myself get this close to him? What would it do to me if I did? Before I could stop myself, I nodded.

Blake didn't wait. He slid his hand into mine. His fingers slipped between mine and his grip tightened. Almost like he wanted people to know that I was his.

But I wasn't his.

I felt so confused. I wanted to pull away. I wanted to demand he take me home where at least my life made sense. Sure, Mom was sick, but I knew that. I could plan for it. But with Blake? Everything was a mess.

As much as I wanted to end this, I knew I was so close to our supposed breakup that I might as well keep going. At the end of this party, Blake would be with Hannah, and I would be alone once more. Sure, that thought made my heart ache, but it also gave me a sense of calm, so I decided to stick it out.

Blake led me through the crowds of people and up to the front door. He never once let go of my hand; instead, he held tighter as we squeezed through the throng of people who were crowding around the entrance of the house and were spilling onto the deck. They were dancing and bobbing their heads to the music.

I had to enact some crazy footwork in order to keep my hand securely in Blake's and avoid all the drinks that people were clinging to while they danced.

Once inside, Blake pulled on my hand so that I could join him by his side. He then led me over to a spot in the corner that had just opened up. I leaned against the wall, and as soon as I realized how close Blake was going to have to stand next to me, I suddenly needed to go outside. But from the way that the crowd had closed in around us, that wasn't going to happen.

"Want me to get you a drink?" Blake leaned closer to me. His warm breath tickled my ear as he dipped his head down to speak into it. His body boxed me in as if he were trying to protect me from those walking by…or that was the only way he could stand in this crowded house. I wasn't sure which one was the reason, and I was fairly certain that I didn't want to know.

Despite my better judgement, I glanced up at him and met his gaze. He looked genuinely worried that I was thirsty. Out of instinct, I bit my lower lip which caused Blake's gaze to drift down to my mouth. Warmth filled my stomach as I watched him study my lips before bringing his gaze back up.

When our gazes met for the second time, my entire body went numb. There was something in the way he looked at me that made my knees weak. Suddenly, all I wanted to do was kiss him. I wanted to feel his body pressed against mine. I wanted to show him how I felt about him.

How I feared I was always going to feel about him.

"Water would be great," I whispered. Even though I wanted him to stay like this, pinning me against the wall, I needed him to leave before I did something incredibly stupid.

"Water?" he asked, his voice was low and husky, and I was fairly certain that if he wasn't standing this close to me, I would have never heard him.

"Water," I repeated.

Blake paused before he pushed away and slipped into the crowd. With him gone, I took in a deep breath, wrapping my arms around my chest and hugging myself. Without his body warmth enveloping me, I felt cold. I also felt incredibly alone. Just like I feared I was going to feel when he picked Hannah over me. When this entire charade was over.

Blake was going to get what he wanted, and me? I would get nothing but a broken heart. I could feel tears start to form on my eyelids, but I blinked a few times to keep them at bay. There was no way I was going to cry at this party, and there was no way I was going to allow myself to cry over Blake.

The only person I allowed myself to cry over is Mom, and I wasn't going to allow myself to stoop so low as to cry over a fake relationship that didn't really matter.

Because it didn't.

I was fairly certain that it didn't matter to Blake, and given enough distance from this situation, it wasn't going to matter to me.

"I'm back."

Blake's voice startled me. I jumped and turned to see him once again, standing inches away from me. He had a cup in one hand and a cookie on a napkin in the other. His eyes were wide from my reaction to which I shot him an apologetic smile.

"Sorry."

He shook his head. "I should be sorry. I didn't mean to startle you."

Feeling claustrophobic and needing to be in a space where I could legitimately step away from Blake, I glanced toward the exit. "I think I need some fresh air," I said as I nodded toward the door.

Blake followed my gesture and then turned to look at me. "Okay."

I didn't wait for him to lead me. Instead, I took off through the crowd. I could feel Blake behind me as I moved, and on occasion, I saw his hand in my peripheral vision as if he were raising his hand to protect me from those around me. My body warmed at the thought of his protecting me, but I didn't allow myself to think too long on it.

I could also be warm from the generated body heat inside of this house. There were a lot of people who were packed in close and dancing.

The cool, evening air hit me as I pushed outside. I took in a deep breath, reveling in the feeling of the difference in temperature. I moved to the far end of the yard, away from the couples making out on the patio furniture and the guys who were playing assorted yard games.

Thankfully, the music and conversations were more muted the farther I went from the house. My ears were ringing, and I shook my head slightly, wishing I could get them to stop. There was a wooden bench tucked in next to a large willow tree. Exhausted, I collapsed on it.

Blake stood a few feet off as if he didn't know where he should go. He glanced around and then moved to sit next to me. I wanted to tell him that I was okay, and if he wanted to, he could leave me here to go find Hannah—but he was sitting before I could stop him.

The relief I felt with him next to me was so powerful that the desire to tell him to leave left me completely.

All I wanted was for him to remain next to me, and I wanted him to feel the same way.

We swung in silence, and I began to wonder why he hadn't left. From what he said earlier today, I thought he wanted me to come, so he could get together with Hannah.

Unable to sit in the unknown any longer, I glanced over at him. "Is Hannah going to be late or something?"

Blake met my gaze. "What?"

I cleared my throat. "Hannah. Do you know where she is?"

He glanced toward the house and then shrugged. He leaned forward on his elbows and stared hard at the ground. "Who knows?" His words were barely a whisper, but I heard them.

"What are you going to tell her?" I needed to keep the focus on Hannah if I was going to survive this party.

"What do you mean?" Blake was now pinching the bridge of his nose. His eyes were closed, and he looked uncomfortable.

"You said that you thought tonight was the night you two would get together. What are you going to say to her to make that happen?" Why hadn't he thought about this? The whole reason for me to come was for them to finally get together, yet it seemed as if he had no plans to make that a reality.

He shrugged. "I don't know." He straightened and leaned against the back of the bench. I could feel his agitation, and it surprised me.

"Wanna go over it with me?"

Blake crossed his arms and stared off in front of us. I wondered if what he was staring at would melt with how hard he was glaring. Then he sighed, his shoulders slumping. "I guess."

Grateful for something to focus on, I turned. "Imagine I'm Hannah."

Blake glanced over at me. He stared at me for a moment before he nodded and shifted to face me like I had done. "Okay."

I waited, but he didn't say anything. "Should I start?"

Blake met my gaze and then shook his head. "I can start."

I nodded and then studied him. There was a part of me that was interested in what he was going to say. Like if I heard the words, then the pain I felt inside would lessen. I would know that Blake was meant to be with Hannah. That he cared for her more than I wanted him to care for me.

Blake looked stoic before he took in a deep breath. "I want you."

My entire body froze as his words washed over me. Somewhere in the back of my mind, I knew they were for Hannah, but the desire to have them mean something for me took over my entire mind, and everything around me slowed. I wasn't sure if I was supposed to react, but I didn't know what I was going to say, so I kept quiet.

"You and I just make sense. We complete each other in ways I never imagined." His voice had turned husky, and I could feel the want in his gaze.

My heart was racing at a speed that I feared would put me into cardiac arrest. All I could see was him, and all I could hear were his words. I knew they were for Hannah, but I needed them to be for me.

"You're the first thing I think about when I wake up in the morning and the last person I want to see when I go to bed at night." His hand wrapped around mine, and I startled but didn't move to pull it back. I wouldn't be able to if I tried. "I think I'm falling in love with you."

His last sentence hung in the air as I stared at him. Did he say that for Hannah...or for me? I thought he was in love with Hannah, so why would he say he was *falling* for her? I parted my lips as I took in the vulnerability of his gaze. As if he'd just bore his heart to me. Me! Susan Jordan.

"Blake," I whispered as every emotion imaginable rushed through me.

His hand moved to cup my cheek, and he leaned in. I knew I should pull back. I knew I should tell him that he did a good job and that there was no way Hannah would turn him down now, but I couldn't. I wanted him. I wanted this.

His lips brushed mine. They were gentle and warm. A sigh escaped my lips making him pull back slightly to meet my gaze. Not wanting him to stop, I grabbed his shirt like it was my lifeline and pulled him back to me.

Hannah or not, I was going to kiss him.

Our lips met again, and this time I didn't hold back. I was going to show him how I felt. How I was certain I was always going to feel. I was at the cliff, and I'd jumped. There was no turning back now.

His hand found its way to my waist, and he pulled me closer. My hands left their post at his chest and slipped up to the nape of his neck where I clung to him. I was falling, and he was the only thing keeping me from plummeting to the earth.

I parted my lips, and he did the same. We deepened the kiss, both exploring and feeling. Everything about him made me feel complete. Everything about him made me feel as if I finally belonged.

We were breathless when we finally pulled apart. My lips felt swollen, and my body, limp. I couldn't meet his gaze at first. I was too scared what I might find there. Was he disappointed? I knew he came here to reconcile with Hannah but kissed me instead.

I wasn't Hannah, and I wasn't sure how Blake felt about that.

I felt his fingers brush my cheek. I glanced up as he tucked my hair behind my ear.

"Are you okay?" he asked. He was frowning as if he feared that he'd done something wrong.

I chewed on my bottom lip. "I don't know," I whispered. Had I done something wrong? What did he think?

Before he could answer, my phone rang. Grateful for the distraction, I hurried to pull it from my purse.

Dad

Panic rose up inside of me. I pressed the talk button and brought the phone to my cheek. "Dad?" My voice cracked. Dad wasn't a phone talker. If he was calling me, something was wrong.

"Susie? It's dad."

I nodded. "I know."

"Your mom fainted. I'm heading with her to the hospital in the ambulance."

I stood, all feeling leaving my body. "Where? What hospital?"

Blake appeared next to me. Tears began to flow as the feelings of guilt and worry rushed over me.

"Glories Bluff General."

I nodded, hoping I didn't forget. "Okay. I'll head over there right now."

Dad didn't say goodbye. Instead, he just hung up, which was okay. I was already stuffing my phone into my purse.

"I need you to take me to the hospital," I said, unable

to meet Blake's eyes. I didn't want to see the pity that I knew was there. I didn't want him to tell me that he was sorry. I just wanted to leave.

I should have been there with Mom, not here, kissing Blake. And certainly not here if Blake didn't feel the same.

Thankfully, he didn't ask me any questions. He just led the way through the house and across the front yard. He took off down the road as soon as I shut the door and buckled.

The ride to the hospital was quiet. Quiet sobs kept escaping my lips, but I couldn't help it. I would never forgive myself if Mom passed, and I wasn't there to tell her I loved her. Or to hear that she loved me one last time.

I should have never left with Blake. I should have stayed home. This whole fake relationship charade needed to end right now.

Blake pulled up into the patient drop off area as soon as we got to the hospital. My hand was already on the door handle, and I was moments away from jumping down.

"Do you want me to wait?" he asked.

I turned to see that Blake looked concerned. His gaze met mine, and I could feel his guilt and worry. Not wanting him to care about me anymore, I shook my head.

"I'm good. I'll just wait with Dad."

I could tell that he wanted to say something more. That he didn't want to leave, but I didn't want him around. I needed him to go.

I needed this to be over.

"Go back to the party. I think what you have planned to tell Hannah is perfect." I jumped out of his truck. I needed the strength that distance was going to give me. "She won't be able to say no."

Blake held my gaze. "You want me to be with Hannah?"

I hated that he looked disappointed, but there was nothing I could do about that. He liked Hannah, not me. And I couldn't live my life for anyone else but Mom now. His plan to get her back had been perfect. I didn't doubt that Hannah would take him back.

"That was the plan, right?" I held his gaze and mustered a relaxed expression.

He swallowed, his Adam's apple bobbing up and down. "I guess."

I smiled and stepped away from his truck. "You'll do great. Good luck."

I didn't wait for him to say anything. Instead, I slammed the door and walked through the sliding doors and into the hospital. It wasn't until I rounded the nearest corner and collapsed against it that I let my tears flow.

My heart was breaking, and there was nothing I could do to stop it.

I was alone.

Again.

15

SUSIE

I don't know how long I sat in the waiting room. Dad had come out and said it might take a few hours to run Mom through the tests, and I told him that I would wait. My head was a complete mess, and my stomach was in turmoil. I wanted to pass out and throw up at the same time.

I couldn't believe that I wasn't there for Mom when she needed me. I couldn't believe that I thought that being with Blake was better than being with Mom. It was my job to take care of her, and I failed.

I would never forgive myself if something happened to her and I missed her last moments with us.

I leaned my elbows onto my knees and studied the ground. Tears brimmed my eyes as the thought that Mom might be slipping away slammed into my skull like a bad dream that I couldn't shake.

I wasn't ready to lose my mom. I had so many things that I wanted to share with her. It wasn't fair.

"How's Mom?"

I glanced up to see Paul standing in front of me. He had on a black hoodie and a stoic expression. He handed me one of the sodas that he was carrying and then plopped down next to me and cracked open the other one.

I wasn't thirsty, but I needed something to do to distract myself, so I opened the bottle and took a sip. The carbonation hit my throat and made me wince, but once I swallowed it, I took another sip. The crispness of the flavor helped ground me, and I was desperate to get a hold of my emotions right now.

"I don't know. Dad said she's awake now, but they are having to run tests on her. He said we could go home, but I told him no."

Paul was studying me as I spoke. He nodded along with my words, silently agreeing that neither of us were going to go anywhere until we could talk to Mom. See with our own eyes that she was okay.

It was the first time in a long time that I actually felt connected to my brother. He'd been so distant lately, and I thought I'd been okay with him feeling far away. I missed this. I missed my brother, and I felt more determined than ever to get to the bottom of his behavior.

If anything, I wondered if this had something to do with Corinne.

Not wanting to attempt to open Pandora's box right

now, I turned and scooted down far enough on the chair so that I could rest my head on the back of the chair. I closed my eyes and forced my mind to clear. I didn't want to think about Paul or what might happen to Mom...and I certainly didn't want to think about Blake—who seemed to want to dominate my every thought.

I finally found a distraction. Instead of thinking about Blake and the feeling of his lips and body against my own, I replayed a Disney movie in my mind. It helped until I felt Paul's elbow jamming into my ribs.

"Dad's coming," he said.

I startled and sat up, glancing around. He was right. The door to the emergency room was shutting, and Dad was headed our direction. I tried to read his expression, but Dad had never been one to read easily.

He walked up to us, and just as he neared, his lips tipped up into a smile. "She's being moved to the oncology unit, but she's okay," he said, relief filling his voice. "They said her blood sugar was too low, and that's why she passed out."

I let out a sob that I didn't know that I was holding as I leapt to my feet to wrap my arms around Dad. Tears began to flow as we embraced. Paul even joined in on the family hug. When I pulled away, Dad's eyes were misty, and Paul was busy focusing on the ground as if he were trying to hide his tears as well.

Dad led us to the oncology unit, and when I saw Mom, my tears started all over again. She gave me an apologetic smile, but I didn't wait for her to say anything. Instead, I crossed the room and wrapped my arms around her.

"I'm so sorry," she whispered. I knew she was tired, and I didn't want her to wear herself out with talking.

"It's okay. I was just worried," I said as I squeezed my eyes shut and just hugged her.

Dad said he was going to get some coffee, and Paul held Mom's hand until he got a phone call and excused himself. I crawled into Mom's bed with her and rested my head on her shoulder. She patted my hand which drew my attention over to her.

"How was the party?" she asked. She managed a small smile.

I swallowed as the memory of what had happened a few hours ago came rushing back to me. I shrugged and shook my head. "We don't have to talk about that right now," I whispered.

Mom leaned farther back, so she could study me. "Did something happen?"

I wanted to tell her everything, but I had a sinking suspicion that she would read into our kiss more than I wanted to. In my mind, Blake and I were just practicing what he was going to say to Hannah, and that was all. There was no feeling behind it on his end. I was the only one who'd gotten caught up in the moment.

It hadn't meant what I wanted it to mean.

"Nothing happened," I lied.

"Susanne Jordan, I was not born yesterday. These

meds may make my mind foggy, but I know you better than anyone else, and it's written all over your face." She leaned into me as she intensified her stare. "Tell your mother."

I giggled, loving that my mom still retained her spunk. It was refreshing and exactly what I needed to feel better about what had happened. But that didn't mean that I wanted to tell her anything.

I patted her hand. "Once you get home, I'll tell you."

She scoffed but I held my ground. Eventually, she gave up when I grabbed the remote and flipped the TV on. We settled on a home improvement channel, laughing at the before photos and oohing and ahhing at the afters.

Eventually, Dad returned and set up camp next to the bed with his readers on and a newspaper spread across his lap. Even Paul came back and settled on the recliner in the corner. He tipped his head back and closed his eyes.

The feeling of our family together once more pulled on my heart strings. I felt so complete, sitting in the hospital room together, that I almost didn't want to leave when Dad woke me up and told me that Paul was going to drive me home. I feared that if I walked through those doors, I was going to have to face reality, and I wasn't ready for that.

Plus, I feared that if I left, something might happen to Mom. I peered over at her before I pulled myself away to see that she was sleeping. Dad assured me that he would watch over her and that she was going to be okay. I still felt unsure, but finally agreed.

The drive home was quiet. By the time I got into the house, exhaustion hit me like a ton of bricks. I was ready to shower and get into bed.

I managed to keep Blake in the farthest regions of my mind up until I pulled my comforter up to my neck and attempted to calm my mind. It was in these moments, the ones where I let my guard down, that his face, his kiss, floated into my mind.

I lay there, forcing my eyes to stay shut as tears began to form once more. This time, it wasn't for Mom, and really, they weren't for Blake.

They were for what I almost had but lost.

They were for what I could never have.

16

SUSIE

School wasn't as hard as I thought it was going to be on Monday. I'd distracted myself all weekend with getting the house unpacked for Mom's return. The doctor said that if all of her levels looked good, she could come home Monday evening.

I cleaned, unpacked, and organized like a mad woman when I wasn't visiting her at the hospital. I was on a mission to forget Blake, and it seemed to be working, until I mistakenly glanced up while I was sitting next to Patty at one of the cafeteria tables, waiting for the first bell to ring, and my gaze met Blake's.

I wanted to look away. I knew I should, but I was stupid, and I held it. He didn't seem in a hurry to look away either. Instead, he sort of paused as he studied me. I wasn't sure how to read his expression, and I wasn't sure I wanted to. I still felt completely confused, and I wasn't in the head space to try to sift through any of it.

Plus, I needed to focus on Mom right now. That was my mission.

So, I pulled my gaze away and focused back on the math homework I was desperate to finish. Patty had kept talking through my moment with Blake, but I hadn't been paying attention and I feared that she was going to ask me a question, so I focused on what she was saying.

Thankfully, she didn't pause as if she were expecting me to react, so I began to relax...until I heard Blake's voice.

"Susie? Can I talk to you?"

My entire body went numb as I glanced up to see Blake standing next to the table. He had his thumb hooked around the shoulder strap of his backpack, and he looked as if he were in pain.

Which only made me feel worse. What had happened after he dropped me off at the hospital Friday night? Had he gone back to the party? Were he and Hannah together?

Where was she?

"Um, sure?" Patty said as she poked me in the ribs in an attempt to get my attention.

I swatted her hand away and turned to focus on Blake. "What do you need?" I asked, hoping that I came off more confident than I felt.

He frowned. "Can I talk to you in private?"

I swallowed against the lump that had formed in my throat. I didn't want to talk to him because I feared what I would do if I did. I wanted Blake more than I thought humanly possible. All of my effort to keep my thoughts clear of him had gone out the window.

I was right back to the pain and regret that I felt when I walked away from him.

"Please?"

I hated that he looked as if he were hurt. I needed him to be happy because at least if he were, that would mean I'd done my job. Now, I just felt like I was failing everyone, and that was a crappy place to be.

"Okay," I said as I shut my math book and shoved it into my backpack. I pushed the chair away from the table and stood, slinging my backpack onto my shoulder.

"I'll see you in English class," Patty called after me.

I gave her a quick wave and then followed Blake into the hallway and over to a row of lockers that were void of any students.

He paused, keeping his back to me for a moment before turning to face me. I wasn't sure what I thought this conversation was going to be about, but I hadn't expected the way he looked at me when he met my gaze.

"Is your mom okay?" he asked.

Relieved that it was just to check on Mom, I nodded. "She's coming home tonight."

He nodded. "That's good." Then he fell silent. He looked as if he wanted to say something but wasn't sure how. "Um…"

"How did it go with Hannah?" I couldn't just stand

here any longer. I needed to move on from this part of my life, and the longer he kept me in the dark about their relationship, the crazier it made me. I needed him to tell me that they were together, so my heart could officially break and I would be able to move on.

"Hannah?"

Why did he look and sound so confused? I nodded. "Yeah. I figured you talked to her after you dropped me off." I folded my arms and studied him. *Just tell me that you are together*, I silently begged.

He furrowed his brow. "I didn't talk to her."

My heart sank. He was waiting. Why was he waiting? Did this mean he wanted to continue this charade? Did he want me to stay his fake girlfriend? I didn't think that I had the strength anymore.

"Susie, I—"

"I don't think you need me anymore. We can just call it quits on our fake relationship." I couldn't hear those words *fake relationship* anymore. The last thing I needed was for him to make his pitch as to why we should continue our fake relationship. It really had reached its inevitable end.

His frown deepened.

"I think you have a great chance with her if you just be you. Tell her how you feel, and she'll take you back. I'm sure of it."

He studied me. "I should just tell her how I feel?"

I nodded. "Be honest, and you'll get far." A soft smile played on my lips. "At least that's what Mom always says."

His expression changed from confusion to a serious one. My heart picked up speed as I watched him take a step forward. Scared at what he might say to me, I took a step back. "I really should get to first period," I whispered.

I didn't want to hear what he had to say. If I was going to protect myself, I needed to distance myself from him. I didn't want to hear an apology, and I certainly didn't want him to thank me for what I did to help him win Hannah back. The last week had meant more to me than him, and anything he said in regard to that would just hurt me.

And I was tired of being hurt.

Thankfully, the bell rang, ripping my gaze from his. I gave him a quick smile and then nodded. "I'll see you later."

I didn't wait for him to respond. Instead, I slipped around the corner of the hallway and hurried down to the next. Once I was sure that he wasn't going to follow me, I leaned against the wall and took in a deep breath, closing my eyes and grounding myself.

I'd never really dated before, so this felt weird. Did I just break up with Blake? Was it a breakup if the relationship wasn't real in the first place? If it hurt this much when I was his fake girlfriend, I could only imagine how it would feel if this had been real.

I was certain it would have broken me.

Gathering my strength, I pulled my body off the wall

and made my way to first period. I dropped into my seat just as the second bell rang. Grateful for the distraction, I turned my attention toward the teacher and lost myself in what she was saying.

I was exhausted by the time Paul pulled into the driveway after school. It was hard forcing myself to keep my attention on my teachers and not allowing my thoughts to drift to Blake, especially when I saw him at lunch. He was sitting with Hannah who looked all too happy to be with him. Blake, on the other hand, looked less than thrilled. He just sat there with his arms crossed and a scowl of his face.

When he caught me looking at him, he dropped his gaze and focused back on Hannah, who was lapping up his attention. I swallowed and turned back to my bland lunch food and Patty's conversation. I loved my best friend, I did, but I was tired of all of this pretending, and I just wanted to go home.

I wanted Mom home.

I pulled open the passenger door and got out. I felt like a zombie as I crossed the yard and into the house. I spent the next two hours cleaning the house and blaring Christmas music. Anything to bring up my spirits before Mom got home.

Dad texted that they were going to pick up dinner before they came home and to expect them home in an hour. I took a long bath and curled up on the couch with a movie to pass the time. I was at the moment a big misunderstanding came up in the romance when Mom and Dad walked into the house. I quickly turned off the TV and stood, letting my blanket fall around me as I crossed the room.

As soon as I got to Mom, I wrapped my arms around her and buried my face into her neck. She smelled a little like a hospital, but overall, I relished in her familiarity.

"I missed you," I whispered as I fought the sob that wanted to escape.

Mom patted my back. "I'm home now, and I'm not going anywhere."

I pulled back and glowered at her. "You'd better not. I can't do this without you."

Mom's smile was weak, but she looked determined. "I promise."

Dad shooed me away from her. He'd brought the Italian food into the kitchen, and he was ready for us to eat. We obeyed as he herded us out of the living room. The room filled with conversation and laughter as we dished up our plates and then moved to sit at the table. Paul was even down in the kitchen, conversing. Which was unlike him.

Ever since Mom went into the hospital, he'd snapped out of whatever funk he'd been in. He looked happier and more fulfilled. It was strange but a relief to see. I'd been missing my brother.

It was the first night in a long time that things felt normal. Mom was laughing, Dad was smiling, and Paul was engaging in conversation. We talked about what happened when Mom was gone—and even embellished a bit just to put on a show. Mom enjoyed it as she laughed and clapped her hands.

After dinner was cleaned up, we made our way to the living room to watch a movie. An age-old tradition in our family. Movie nights had been a regular growing up. Mom always went all out with fancy popcorns and candy. We'd fight over what movie to watch to which Mom would just declare it a marathon night.

I missed this.

I let Paul pick the movie since he was making an effort. Plus, I was just happy to have Mom home, and I was content to sit next to her and enjoy her company. Mom wrapped her arm around me, and I snuggled in next to her. Being next to Mom helped heal my heart...sort of. I still hurt over Blake, but the Mom-sized hole that had been created when she left had been filled. And I was going to enjoy that for as long as I could.

"How are things with Blake?" Mom asked, halfway through the movie.

I winced at her question. I'd been hoping she wouldn't bring it up. I pulled back and gave her a quizzical look as if playing dumb was what I needed to do to distract her.

She held her ground. "Is he back with Hannah?"

Suddenly, tears began to fall. I tried to keep them at bay, but I was tired. Tired of pretending that I wasn't hurting. Tired of pretending that I didn't love Blake. That I didn't want him around.

Mom's expression softened as she pulled off her blanket and took my hand. "Sus and I are going to refill the popcorn bowl," she called over her shoulder as she led me into the kitchen and away from Dad and Paul who didn't even look up.

She led me over to the nearest barstool and pushed on my shoulders to sit. I obeyed. Then, she stood in front of me with her arms folded and a no nonsense look on her face.

"Tell me everything."

I paused, gathering the courage to speak, and then I told her everything. How much time we'd spent together. How it felt to be next to him. The kiss. I told her that we'd grown close and that I'd fallen for him, but he still wanted Hannah.

I told her that I was hurt.

Mom listened. She didn't speak much while I talked. Instead, she just absorbed. By the time I was done, I was exhausted and hunched over my body. I'd stopped crying a while ago—I doubted I had any tears left. I'd spent so long crying over Mom and Blake, that I was certain that I'd tapped that resource.

Suddenly, Mom's arms were around me and she was hugging me. I froze for a second before I returned the hug, burying my face in her shoulder.

"I'm so sorry, Susie," she whispered as she patted my

back. "If I'd known this would happen, I would have never suggested it." She pulled back, so she could look me in the eye as she tucked some hair behind my ear. "I wanted you to have some fun. You spend so much time with me, that I hoped this would help you get out a bit."

Her eyes misted with tears. "I want you to have a normal teenage life."

I smiled, nodding at her words. "I know. I don't blame you. I'm the loser who couldn't keep her feelings at bay."

Mom shook her head. "You're not a loser." Then her expression turned serious. "Did you tell Blake how you felt?"

My body turned cold at that thought. "No." There was no way I was going to admit to Blake how I felt. There was no way he would return that sentiment, and I didn't want to put myself out there like that.

I couldn't be hurt again.

Mom frowned. "Then you don't know if he feels the same."

I scoffed. "There's no way."

Mom stared at me as if I'd just slandered our family name. "What are you talking about? Boys don't just kiss girls like you said. Besides, I've seen him around you. There's a definite attraction there."

"Gross, Mom."

We both startled and turned to see Paul standing in the doorway with the empty popcorn bowl. He glanced between us with his nose wrinkled. "I'm just going to pretend you didn't just say that about my best friend and my kid sister."

Mom waved away his comment and turned to face me. "Listen to your mother. I've been around longer than him." She shot Paul a death stare.

Paul didn't seem to notice as he crossed the room and grabbed a popcorn bag from the box. He opened it and unfolded it before slipping it into the microwave. While the microwave hummed to life, he turned to face us. "Blake is a stand-up guy. He wouldn't just lead you on for fun."

I tapped the counter, wondering if I should bring up Corinne. Did Paul know about that? "What about Corinne?" I asked before I could stop myself.

Paul froze, his expression falling. He had not expected me to mention her.

"Cori?" he asked.

I nodded. "Patty told me how he led her on."

Paul's focus shifted to something over my shoulder as if he lost himself in thought. Then, he softly shook his head and turned his attention back to me. "Patty doesn't know the whole story. Blake was a stand-up guy in that situation as well."

I frowned. "How?"

"Yeah, what's the story there?" Mom moved to stand next to me so that we were both facing Paul now.

"It's not a big deal," Paul said just as the microwave

beeped. He pulled out the bag by holding gingerly to one corner and then shook it out.

Mom gave him a stern look to which he sighed and moved to set the popcorn bag on the counter next to the bowl. "It's not a big deal. We both met her. She liked Blake. I liked her..." His voice trailed off as an all too familiar scowl returned to his face. "It wasn't Blake's fault. As soon as he knew that I had feelings, he stepped away."

"That's why he broke it off with her," I whispered.

"They were dating?" Mom asked. The tone of her voice told me that she was thoroughly confused.

"Not really. Flirting. You know, the way Blake acts with everyone."

I nodded. I knew that all too well. But there was a thought, back in the hollows of my mind that told me, it wasn't just flirting with me. Not anymore.

"He's a good guy, Susie. And he wouldn't lead you on. Not like that." Paul looked pained as he spoke the words. As if he really didn't want to say that about his best friend. Paul may have been distant from us, but he was loyal.

"Is that why you've been so crabby? Because you miss Corinne?" I teased.

Paul paused, and his smile turned into a frown. It made me feel bad for even mentioning it.

"You're going through a heart break right now. Don't fault me for mine."

I slipped off the barstool and headed over to my

brother. We were more similar than I thought. I pulled him into a hug. "You deserve better."

Paul hesitated for a moment before he squeezed me back. "Thanks. I'll be fine," he whispered.

We separated, and Mom cheered. I turned to face her, and the tears that she'd been holding back were now flowing. "That's my kids."

Paul groaned while I took a bow. He finished opening the popcorn bag and dumped the contents into the bowl. He carried it past us, muttering "crazy people" as he passed by.

I just grinned at him, patting his shoulder when he neared. That just made him move faster, and a moment later, I was alone in the kitchen with Mom. She turned her focus on me, and suddenly, I wanted to hightail it out of here like my brother.

She looked like a woman on a mission, and I had a sinking suspicion that right now, I was her mission.

"What are you scheming?" I asked, hesitantly.

Mom clapped her hands. "The greatest plan ever."

17

SUSIE

I'm not sure why Mom had looked so devious when she pitched her plan to me, but she did. I couldn't help but think that she was taking some sort of joy out of this. And honestly, as much as I feared her plan and what it might do to my heart, I loved seeing Mom so engaged.

I was going to revel in this moment with her.

The plan was simple. I was going to go over to Blake's house, and I was going to tell him how I felt. Mom said something about standing outside of his window with a boom box, but I put a kibosh on that idea. I didn't think Blake would appreciate that. Especially if things were strained at his house.

But I did like the idea of going over and having a conversation. After all, there was no way I could spend the rest of the school year feeling like this. I needed to address what had happened between us, face my feelings, and start to heal if he said no.

At least then, I would know.

But it was scary. Mom helped me see that I was going to be okay. She instructed that I go upstairs, change out of my clothes and into something a bit nicer, and then she'd have some anxiety-relieving tea for me when I got down.

My tiny makeover montage didn't take too long. I got back down to the kitchen in a matter of minutes. Call it my nerves, but I dressed much quicker that I'd ever done. I was wearing a black pair of leggings and a long maroon shirt. I pulled my hair back and applied a bit of makeup—just so I didn't look like I'd been crying.

The herbal tea that Mom had heated up was steaming from the mug. I moved to grab it, taking a sip. Instant bitterness hit my tongue. I pulled it away from me so that I could look down at the murky water.

"What is this?" I asked, wrinkling my nose.

"It'll help with your anxiety."

I smacked my tongue a few times before trying it again. Same bitter taste assaulted my senses. "Nope. Can't do that," I said, setting the mug back down. Thankfully, this conversation helped distract me for a moment and my anxiety did lessen—until I remembered what I was going to do, and the fear washed over me like a wave.

Mom grabbed the mug and sniffed it. Then she shrugged and took a sip. "You're loss."

I shook my head as I grabbed a soda from the fridge

and popped the top. After washing the taste of the tea from my mouth, I leaned against the counter. Nothing was going to calm my nerves.

"You'll be fine. Blake will be kind," Mom said after taking a big sip of the tea.

I nodded. "I know. I've just...never done something like this before."

Mom crossed the room and wrapped me into a hug. "You'll do beautifully. That's part of living. Putting your heart out there without knowing what might happen is the definition of having lived. And you'll do it beautifully."

It felt nice, hugging Mom. It made all of my fear and concerns sort of melt away. She did have a point. Life wasn't worth living if you didn't take a chance now and again. If I wanted closure, I was going to have to face this. Blake and Paul were still friends. I was going to see Blake on occasion, and the last thing I wanted was to worry about one more thing in my life.

I gathered my courage and pulled away. I gave Mom a soft smile and stepped back. She patted my arm and then turned just as Dad walked into the kitchen.

"I was watching a movie, and suddenly, my entire family disappeared," he said as he crossed the room and wrapped his arm around Mom's shoulders. She leaned into him, and the sight in front of me made me smile.

My parents were in love and adorable. And it made me want something like that for myself someday.

"Susie and I were just talking. She's got an errand to run, but I'll come back in with you."

Dad shot me a confused look, but before he could ask me where I was going or why, Mom ushered him out of the kitchen. Just before she disappeared around the corner, she shot me one last encouraging smile.

I offered her a weak one back and then grabbed my purse and keys from the counter and hurried out the side door.

The drive to Blake's house felt shorter than it had in the past. I was so lost in my thoughts of what I was going to say that I was startled when I pulled into his driveway and turned off my lights. Dusk had settled around his farm, and there was only a faint light on inside his house.

As I stared at the darkness in front of me, I began to worry that he wasn't even here. That I'd mustered all the courage I had and drove here for nothing. Not wanting to leave without at least trying, I pulled my keys from the ignition and set them in my purse. I opened the car door and stepped out onto the gravel.

It felt wrong interrupting the silence that surrounded me with a slammed door, so I shut it quietly. I wrapped my arms around my chest and headed toward his front door, praying that this wasn't the start of some nineties teen murder mystery.

I was standing on his porch, ready to ring the doorbell, when a hand reached out and wrapped around my arm. I yelped and turned only to be met with Blake's scowl. It took a moment for my racing heart to finally slow. I parted my lips to speak, but Blake beat me to it.

"What are you doing here?" he asked. His voice was low and harsh, but I could see pain in his gaze. He had a gash on his forehead that was covered in dried blood and his eye was swollen. I'd seen him excuse away the previous injuries, and I wondered how he was going to explain these new ones.

"Did your dad hit you again?" I asked as I stepped closer to him to see his injuries. I reached up to touch his cut, but then stopped when I realized just how hard Blake was staring at me.

"Why are you here?" he asked again. There was a desperation in his voice that caught me off guard.

"I, um…" What was I supposed to say? I had everything rehearsed in the car, but it didn't feel appropriate to say them now. "I was worried about you."

Blake frowned, and then suddenly, he slipped his hand that had been holding my arm down and into my hand. Then he pulled me off his deck, across his yard, and into his barn.

Once we were safely inside, he shut the door and turned on the lamp in the corner. He pulled me over to an overturned bucket and I sat. He began to pace in front of me, pushing his hand through his hair as he moved.

"You shouldn't have come," he mumbled.

I glared at him. "You need to leave. If your dad is doing this to you, you need to report him."

Blake paused and glanced over at me. "What?"

I sighed. "This is not right. You need to stand up for yourself."

Blake scoffed. "And go where? I have no other place to go."

"Come to our house."

"Your house?"

I knew I was committing a lot by saying this, but I was fairly certain that Mom and Dad wouldn't mind. Especially when they found out what his dad had been doing to him. "They see you like a son. They won't have a problem."

Blake stopped moving and stared at me. "What about you?"

My mouth went dry. "What about me?" The intensity in his stare never let up. It was all I could see and all I could feel.

"What do you see me as?"

All words left my brain. I wanted to speak, to say something intelligent, but I couldn't think of anything except three little words. Three words I'd never said to anyone but that I wanted to say to him.

The whole reason I'd come here in the first place.

He stepped closer to me. "What do you see me as?" he asked again, his voice deepening with each word.

I glanced up at him. I was scared. I wanted to say the words, to tell him how I feel, but what if he was with Hannah now? What if he didn't care?

"Susie?" he asked again.

"How's Hannah?" The words tumbled out of my mouth before I could stop them.

Blake paused before turning and pushing his hand through his hair once more. "No clue. I told her we were done and to leave me alone."

My whole body went numb. "You what?" I asked.

He glanced over at me. "I realized that I don't want Hannah. She's not the person who I want to be with. To be around."

My heart began to pound. "She's not?"

He shook his head as he took a step closer to me. "She's not."

I swallowed as I stared at him. "Who do you want?"

His gaze intensified. "I'm worried she doesn't want me back."

"You are?" My heart was pounding harder and harder with each word.

He nodded. "I fell for her, hard. But she keeps walking away from me. I'm worried that if I tell her how I feel, she'll leave for good."

"Maybe she won't," I said with a slight shrug to my shoulders.

"She won't?"

I shook my head. "She won't."

Blake was in front of me now. He reached down and grabbed my waist, pulling me up. His lips found mine, and he crushed me against his chest as he held me. He kissed me.

A sob escaped my lips, and my body filled with joy. I wrapped my arms around him. There was no way I was going to let him go ever again.

He pulled me up, and I wrapped my legs around him. He walked forward until my back was pressed against the wall of the barn. I parted my lips as we deepened the kiss. My heart pounded, and I was sure he could feel it. I never wanted to let him go. I wanted this…forever.

When Blake finally lowered me to the ground and pulled away, I felt lightheaded and faint. He kept me boxed in next to the wall, and his forehead was pressed against mine.

I rested my hands on his chest where I could feel his heart pounding just like mine.

"I'm glad you came for me," he whispered.

I glanced up to meet his gaze. "Me too."

He pulled back. "Why did you come?"

I studied him. "To tell you that I love you."

He furrowed his brow. "You do?"

I nodded. "But I was scared that you only saw me as your fake girlfriend."

Blake dipped down and pressed his lips to mine. The kiss was soft and gentle and fulfilled me in a way that I didn't think was possible. "You stopped being fake a long time ago."

"I did?"

He nodded. "You mean the world to me." He pressed his lips against mine once more. "I love you, too."

I'm not sure how long we sat in the barn talking, but time felt so abstract when I was with him. Eventually, Mom texted asking for an update, so I moved to stand, brushing the straw off my butt. "Come on," I said, holding out my hand for him.

Blake stood and wrapped his hand in mine. "Where are we going?"

I gave him a soft smile as I lead him out of the barn. "Home."

"Home?"

I nodded. "I'm getting you out of this place. We're going to ask Mom and Dad if you can move in."

He paused. "Do you really think that's a good idea?"

I scoffed as I pulled open the driver's side door. "Do you think it's bad?"

Blake paused as he stared at me. Then he shrugged. "Nope."

We held hands the entire ride to my house. When we got inside, it only took a few minutes to convince Mom and Dad that living in the apartment above the garage was the best thing for Blake. Luckily, he was eighteen and could legally move out of his parent's house.

The smile on Blake's face made me feel like I was flying. He was happy. Mom was healthy. And my family was complete.

I don't know what I did to deserve this, but I was going to take it.

For now, my life was complete.

I couldn't ask for anything more.

***

I hope you enjoyed Rule #7. I loved writing Susie and Blake's romance.

Up next, is Charlotte and Lucas' story. Lucas has been banished to the small town of Sweet Creek by his rich father who wants him to learn a thing or two. Poor Charlotte is just trying to survive her mom's passing. They start out as enemies to lovers, but soon realize, they had more in common than they thought.

You'll love reading how they break the rules of love in *Rule #8: You Can't Excuse the Billionaire's Heir* HERE!

Want more Rule of Love Romances?? Head on over and grab you next read HERE.

For a full reading order of Anne-Marie's books, you can find them HERE.

Or scan below:

Printed in Great Britain
by Amazon